Daughters of the Sun

A Winter at St-Tropez

by

Bill MacDonald

To Don & Kathy —

Bill MacDonald

nov/03

Daughters of the Sun

A Winter at St-Tropez

by

Bill MacDonald

"The sun god Apollo (also known as Helios, or, in Roman mythology, Sol) drives his four-horse chariot daily across the Heavens. He is not only god of the sun, but of music, poetry, prophecy and all the fine arts. His several herds of sacred cattle are tended by his daughters, Phaetusa and Lampetia."
—Robert Graves: *The Greek Myths*

Borealis Press Ltd.
Ottawa, Canada
2003

Canadä

*The Publishers acknowledge the financial assistance
of the Government of Canada through the Book Publishing
Industry Development Program (BPIDP)
for our publishing activities*

National Library of Canada Cataloguing in Publication Data

MacDonald, Bill, 1932-
    Daughters of the sun: a winter at St-Tropez / Bill MacDonald.

ISBN 0-88887-226-7

    I. Title.

PS8575.D668D38 2003   C813'.54   C2003-900491-0
PR9199.3.M3115D38 2003

Cover design by Bull's Eye Design, Ottawa
Book typesetting by Chisholm Communications, Ottawa
Photos by Bill MacDonald

Printed and bound in Canada on acid-free paper

Daughters of the Sun

Table of Contents

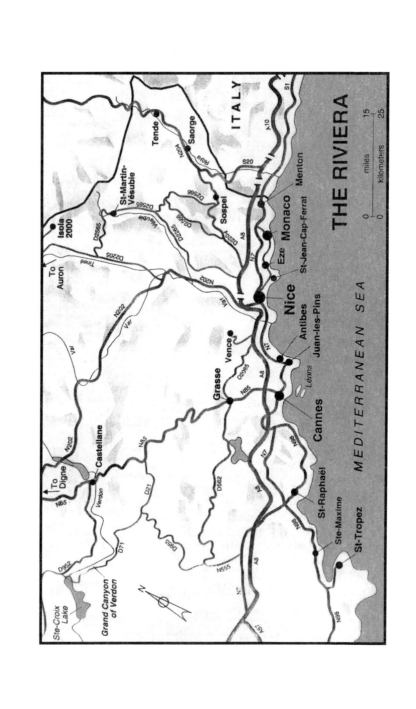

THE RIVIERA

ITALY

Tende
Saorge
St-Martin-Vésuble
Isola 2000
To Auron
Sospel
Menton
Eze Monaco
St-Jean-Cap-Ferrat
Nice
Antibes
Juan-les-Pins
Vence
Lerins
Grasse
Cannes
Castellane
To Digne
St-Raphaël
Ste-Maxime
St-Tropez
Grand Canyon of Verdon
Ste-Croix Lake

MEDITERRANEAN SEA

N

miles 0   15
kilometers 0   25

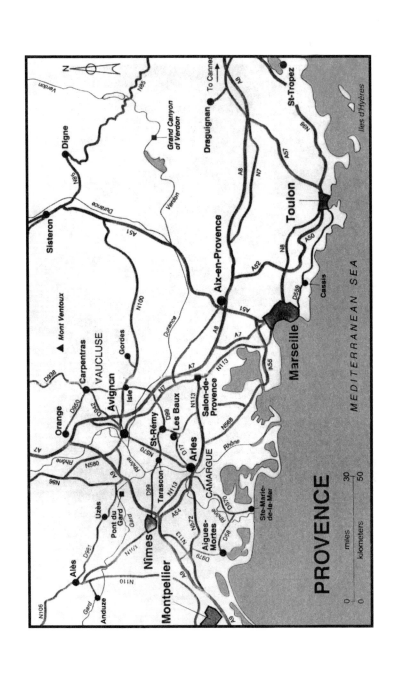

PROVENCE

Plessi Toussaint

Chapter One

If you want to sunbathe and see famous people, winter is the wrong time of year to be in St-Tropez. The Côte d'Azur is all but deserted. In December, alpine winds gust down from the Moorish Hills. In January, seas run high between Cap Fréjus and Cap des Sardinaux. As late as March, rain squalls sweep inland under scudding clouds. On a day like today, cars splash by with their headlights on and their windows rolled up. Children on their way to school wear yellow slickers. Unsmiling pedestrians carry umbrellas and stride along purposefully, puddle-hopping, where normally they'd saunter. Most noticeably, the café crowd is meagre. Bars and restaurants are sparsely populated. Here at Le Gorille, which at this hour in summer is packed with aperitif-drinkers, only six other tables are occupied.

Sipping my third or fourth rum grog, trembling only slightly, it occurs to me that there is no more depressing place than a sidewalk café in the rain. It was surely in just such a setting that someone coined that expression, "Le roi est mort, vive le roi!" (The king is dead, long live the king!) On sunny days, surrounded by strangers, one takes comfort in the babble of voices, the shouts, the laughter. But in the rain, one feels lonely, ostracized. Perhaps a little desperate. There are no distractions, no excuses for levity, and so one must face facts. To combat this, one orders yet another rum grog. As Marius the surly waiter departs, muttering about stupid Anglais who sit outdoors in such weather, one lights a fresh Gauloise, sucks the smoke in deep, and implores one's hands to stop trembling. For comfort, one reaches into one's pocket and pulls out a recently purchased train ticket. Provided one has a safe place to go and the means to travel, escape may be the best defence.

I've been here six months now. When I arrived in October, the summer hordes were already dispersing. Yachts at the marina were being mothballed for winter. People had fled to Cannes, or Nice, or Monaco. Cruise ships, bound from Genoa to the Caribbean, steamed by without stopping. My new Swiss friends, Dinard and Pascaline, with whom I'd shared a compartment on the train from Marseille, were totally disillusioned. They said there was nothing to do. They'd counted on visiting Brigitte Bardot at her home in the Moorish Hills. No such luck. The gate on her electrified fence was padlocked, her villa shuttered. Woody Allen was alleged-ly giving clarinet lessons downtown at Bistro des Lices. Not true. Rumour had it that Julia Roberts was at Hôtel Byblos on her honeymoon. She wasn't. So after three days of com-plaining, Dinard and Pascaline left by bus for Monte Carlo. Dinard said they'd be back at Christmas, but he lied. I suspect they went on up to Basel, where Pascaline has relatives.

My intention was to stay a month, see if I could draw inspiration enough to begin a novel. My most recent book, *Crown of Wild Olives*, had sold well enough to finance a win-ter of cheap lodgings on the Riviera. It was something I'd always wanted to do, but until now, couldn't afford. Unlike Dinard and Pascaline, I had no wish to encounter movie stars. I did hope to discover the ghost of that famous French author, Guy de Maupassant, who made St-Tropez his home in the late 1880s. Back then, it was still an unspoilt coastal village. Battling insanity, de Maupassant took refuge in a gar-ret on quai Suffren and wrote ten chapters of *Bel Ami*, the novel that predicted with chilling accuracy his own death in a Paris asylum.

I had one more reason for wanting to spend time in St-Tropez. My Canadian publisher, Borealis Press, had recently acquired North American translation rights to Plessi Tous-saint's scandalous book, *Crédillon*. (You may recall the full page ad in the *Globe & Mail*, announcing that *Crédillon* had just won the coveted Prix Médici.) According to Borealis, Plessi, a notorious drunk and womanizer, whose previous best sellers had already cost his French publisher, Gallimard, a fortune in libel suits, was secretly wintering in St-Tropez. They said he was hiding from hit men, living the life of a recluse, working on a new book that would expose the extramarital shenanigans of several high-ranking French politicians, including President Jacques Chirac and Prime Minister Alain Juppé. My Borealis editor, Nicole Cléry, informed me that Plessi Toussaint was holed up in a St-Tropez apartment on quai Suffren, above a book, bag and umbrella shop, called Filles du Soleil. It was Nicole's understanding that the proprietor of Filles du Soleil (*Daughters of the Sun*), who owned the entire tenement, offered rooms at winter rates to writers and artists. She said that F. Scott Fitzgerald had resided there in the fall of 1926, vainly attempting a sequel to *The Great Gatsby*, coming up instead with a plan for *Tender is the Night*. She said that if I were to present myself to the concierge, a certain Monsieur Nemours, and mention Fitzgerald, or even de Maupassant, I might be accommodated.

Which in due course I was. They gave me a bare, drafty, one-room apartment on the second floor. My fair weather friends, Dinard and Pascaline, who abhorred the grunge of Filles du Soleil, took a room instead at Hotel Sube, above the Café de Paris, on quai Jean-Jaurès. Not surprisingly, they weren't happy there. For one thing, it was twice as expensive as Filles du Soleil. For another, it was very noisy. For yet another, the manager, a man named Rance, brother-in-law of my landlord, Monsieur Nemours, entered their room any time of the day or night without knocking. Worst of all, the television set had only two channels. So I wasn't surprised when they said they were leaving. They had no interest in Guy de Maupassant, nor in F. Scott Fitzgerald, nor in Plessi Toussaint. They knew that Fitzgerald and de Maupassant were dead, thought Plessi Toussaint soon would be. On Allhallows Eve, after a farewell dinner at Brasserie la Jetée and a promise of postcards, they set out for Monte Carlo. I didn't realize it at the time, but they took with them the only Toussaint books I owned—paperback translations of *La Roukerie*

(*The Rookery*) and *Jocrisse* (*The Simpleton*). Nicole Cléry had given them to me as a going-away present. I'd not yet read either of them, and regretted lending them out.

I believe it was the very next morning that I first saw Plessi Toussaint. I was enjoying coffee and a Gauloise at Le Gorille, or it might have been at La Marine, across the street, when I noticed a sombre, plump little man, in brown hat and dark jacket, wearing spectacles and bright blue socks. He was sitting alone, looking bored, or fatigued, yawning his head off. I watched him rip apart a Gauloises cigarette packet, which was obviously empty, crumple it in disgust, and throw it on the floor. Finally he picked up the newspaper he'd been reading and began sipping from a steaming glass of rum grog. Over the newspaper, our eyes met. Raindrops had gathered along the brim of his brown hat, and now ran off onto his shoulders. He looked annoyed, but made no move to go indoors. I admired him for that. From the description Nicole Cléry had given me, I was pretty sure this was the brilliant Plessi Toussaint, though I must admit I'd been expecting a handsomer man. He was clean-shaven, had a sour, rather dissolute air about him. His was not a face you could imagine smiling much. His eyes seemed sad, rather haunted, as though he had insoluble problems. He wore brown leather shoes that matched his hat, and though his jacket was quilted and possessed a collar, the mulled grog he was sipping failed to bring colour to his cheeks. I certainly wouldn't have taken him for the prize-winning author of *Crédillon*, a truly salacious novel detailing the aberrant sex lives of Benoit Cotte, mayor of Paris, and Bernardin Thibault, secretary-general of the railway union. I'd tried to read *Crédillon* in the original French, but found it difficult, gross, offensive. It seemed to be a raw mixture of Henry Miller's *Tropic of Capricorn*, D.H. Lawrence's *The Rainbow*, and Comte de Sade's *Days of Sodom*. (Interestingly, those three men were all prosecuted for obscenity, but Plessi Toussaint, who should have been, wasn't.)

In my view, writers who pen such books, if male, should be tall, gaunt, darkly bearded. They should wear sunglasses in public to disguise themselves from assassins and autograph-seekers. Except for his clenched jaw and peevishness, Plessi Toussaint looked more like an office manager or indolent civil servant.

I stood up, walked over to his table, offered him a Gauloise. With scarcely a glance, and not a word, he accepted one, stuck it between his lips, allowed me to light it for him. He inhaled deeply, took a long sip from his glass of grog and went back to reading *Le Monde*.

"Je vous en prie, Monsieur Toussaint," I said sarcastically, and returned to my table.

As I was finishing my coffee, a gust of wind huffed down the street, showering us with drizzle. From where I sat, I could see the grey stone lighthouse at the harbour entrance. Men on a scaffold were patching its red upper section, and at that exact moment, for unknown reasons, its beacon began flashing. Which seemed silly, because even had there been any boat traffic, it was broad daylight. I thought about asking Plessi Toussaint for an explanation, and would have done so, as a way of opening the conversation, but when I turned around, he was gone. His newspaper and empty glass were still there, and the cigarette I'd given him was smouldering in the ashtray, but of him, there was no sign. I remember feeling vaguely abandoned and wondering whether I should have gone east with Dinard and Pascaline. Just then Marius, the surly waiter, handed me my tab, and Plessi Toussaint's as well. "What's this?" I said.

"Zee gentlemans at zis table say you will pay eez grog for eem, monsieur."

"I can't imagine what gave him that idea. I don't even know the man."

Marius shrugged, glared at me. He was impatient to be back inside where it was warm and dry, where there were sociable folk and electric heaters. I felt my temper rising. "See here, I don't go around paying other people's bar tabs."

"He say you will, monsieur. He call you eez copain."

"But I don't even know his name!"

"Eez name eez Plessi Toussaint, monsieur. He is the famous writer from Paris. He say you are eez copain."

"Well, I'm not his copain. And if I were, he's the one who should be paying, not me."

"Ah, monsieur, maybe tomorrow he pay. Today, he have no money, no cigarette. When he have money, he pay."

By now, people were staring out the window at us, laughing. Determined not to be intimidated, I ordered another café crème and drank it slowly, nonchalantly. I smoked two more cigarettes. Overhead, there were breaks in the cloud. The sun was actually trying to shine. Two stout women with white poodles on leashes walked by. Both dogs veered toward me, started sniffing my shoes. Conversing intently, the women waited until the dogs were ready to continue. Feeling victimized and foolish, I summoned Marius, gave him ten Euros, beat an ignoble retreat toward the Filles du Soleil. What infuriated me was that as I approached, I saw Plessi Toussaint standing on the balcony of his third floor apartment. He was leaning on the railing, looking down at me. He had removed his dark jacket but was still wearing his brown hat. As I stared up at him, he turned and went indoors, anxious, no doubt, to get on with his latest scandalmongering.

During our first real literary discussion, over breakfast at Le Gorille about a week after my arrival, I learned that Plessi Toussaint, like Guy de Maupassant and Marcel Proust, did most of his writing at night. The morning I offered him a cigarette and paid his tab, he'd been on his way to bed. His routine, he said, was to sleep all day, get up at dusk, and work at his word processor till midnight. Since he kept no food in his apartment (Monsieur Nemours forbade it), he'd then go down to Le Gorille for a plate of bouillabaisse and a carafe of wine. Then, unless he had visitors or a party to attend, back to the word processor till dawn, fuelled by cigarettes and black tea brewed in an electric kettle. When the sun came up, or his eyes fell shut, he would stumble down to Le Gorille again, order a cheese omelet, read the morning paper. Sometimes, he said, he would fall asleep at the table. But what he liked to do was smoke a Gauloise, drink a grog and an espresso, think about the next night's writing. His exhausted brain, he said, stimulated by tobacco, alcohol and caffeine, sometimes served up outrageous imagery, gave him unique ideas. If this occurred, he would hurry back to his apartment and record the ideas before they evaporated. When I asked him why he didn't bring paper and pencil to breakfast, he threw up his hands in horror and called me a "rustaud stupide"—a stupid rube.

As we tucked into our croissants, I learned other things too. I learned that he was fluent in English because he'd lived in London. His first job had been as a teacher of conversational French at a Wembley girls' school. After being dismissed for improper conduct, he'd worked as night reporter on several London newspapers, among them the *Daily Telegraph*, the *Guardian* and the *Evening Standard*. The best, he said, had been the *Evening Standard*, whose editor-in-chief, a woman named Langtry, had asked him to do a feature on French attitudes toward the Beatles. She frequently took him out for breakfast at Admiral Duncan's in Soho. Which was rather surprising, he said, because Ms Langtry was a dyed-in-the-wool lesbian. Speaking of which, did I know a female editor at Borealis Press in Ottawa by the name of Nicole Cléry?

I said I did. In fact, I knew her well. It was she who had edited my *Crown of Wild Olives* and told me that Plessi was hibernating in St-Tropez.

"She's a lesbian too," Plessi said.

"Who is?"

"Nicole Cléry, your lady editor at Borealis."

"Oh, I don't think so. I mean, that's the first I've heard of it."

"Trust me, mon gars, she is."

"How can you be so sure?"

"She told me."

"I suppose you made a move on her?"

"No, I ask her can she put me in touch with a professional lesbian who will validate my manuscript. She say there is nobody more expert than her, which I believe."

"Well, live and learn," I said. "I would never have guessed."

"Which mean, mon gars, that you are grossièrement malappris—offensively boorish."

That morning, I chalked his rudeness up to fatigue. I didn't yet know how typical it was. True, he'd spent the whole night writing and it had not gone well. He'd done twenty pages, deleted six. At that rate, his new book would take forever. He'd already spent his publisher's advance, was due back in Paris with the manuscript at Easter. He admitted he was in a bad mood. What he needed, he said, was a night of debauchery, of drinking with friends at Brasserie La Jetée, to recharge his batteries. Except that he had few friends outside Paris. Few real friends. In fact, he had none. The novelist's life was a lonely one. In Paris, he could live well, but couldn't write. In St-Tropez, he could write well, but couldn't live. Which was why they'd sent him here. That and to protect him from vengeful dignitaries. What he planned to do after breakfast was visit young Yvette Chanteloup, a waitress down the street at Crêperie Bretonne, and have his ashes drawn. Yvette, he said, a big girl who serviced special customers on a couch in the back of her establishment, had given him a ten o'clock appointment. He hoped he could stay awake till then. Perhaps, he said, Mademoiselle Chanteloup could unblock his brain and restore him. She'd done it before, using skills unfamiliar to most women. Should he make an appointment for me as well? A referral was needed. You couldn't just walk in off the street. I said I'd take a rain check.

Despite his acid tongue, I enjoyed Plessi's company those early autumn mornings at Le Gorille. I respected him as a writer of best sellers, admired his work ethic, his self-discipline. His reliance on sedatives and stimulants was understandable, even forgivable.

On occasion, when people he didn't like hounded him for his autograph, we would flee Le Gorille and go down the street to his second favourite hangout, Le Relais des Coches. The waiter's name there was Leon and he made sure no one bothered Plessi. Not even those who recognized him from photographs on his book jackets, or from articles about him in *Paris Match*. "Some assholes," Plessi would say, "won't leave you alone, even at breakfast, which to me is as sacred a ceremony as taking a shit. If I have a gun, I shoot the bastards."

I must admit, Plessi Toussaint taught me the joys of starting the day with mulled rum. One or two with breakfast, he said, would keep you mellow till lunchtime. If you needed your wits about you, a third was inadvisable. For him, on his way to bed, or to visit Yvette Chanteloup, it didn't matter. He could go ahead and indulge. Sometimes, if he feared insomnia, he might even quaff a fourth. Never a fifth, though, because that would risk nightmares and a hangover. A little red wine with the evening meal, a snifter of Cointreau to clear the cobwebs, a drop of Pernod in your tea. For headache, unlimited aspirin. For constipation, six ripe pears with milk of magnesia. For bad dreams or lack of initiative, a morning visit to Mademoiselle Chanteloup. "To be a writer," he said, "a successful writer, is to live in limbo. There is no worse fate. You cannot have friends, for fear you use them in your books. You cannot have a wife, a family, a mistress. Think of the great André Gide, as queer as they come. Think of poor Flaubert, or the pitiful Marcel Proust. Think of Balzac, Zola, the profligate Georges Simenon. You know what is a profligate? This is a man like me, a swinger, many times married but never churched. To be a serious writer, like Céline, like Baudelaire, the sacrifice is enormous. Plus the risk of madness. If you are not crazy to begin with, you soon will be. You may resort to suicide, if someone doesn't kill you first. Or you may drink yourself to death. Or, like Rimbaud, die of drugs and disease. Better to enter a monastery, or live under a bridge in Paris. Here in St-Tropez, at Les Filles du Soleil, I live like a monk anyway, in my Cro-Magnon cave, with etchings of extinct animals on the walls. By the way, have you read my books?"

"Only *Crédillon*, I'm afraid, and only in English. I had copies of *Jocrisse* and *La Roukerie*, but unfortunately I lent them to friends on the train and never got them back."

He looked at me with raised eyebrows. "*Crédillon*? Really? Are you certain? I was unaware it had been translated. I'm surprised I wasn't notified. So, tell me, what did you think?"

"I enjoyed it immensely. I look forward to reading your other books, first chance I get."

"In English, of course."

"Well, yes, in English. Otherwise, I miss too much."

"I'm sure you do. In St-Tropez, you may not find my books in English. If you do, save your money, mon gars. I've heard they're abominably translated."

Chapter Two

In November, to placate Marius, we began having breakfast indoors at Le Gorille. We sometimes met there in the evening too, before Plessi started his night's work. On occasion, we even shared a plate of scallops at midnight. At all these meals, though Plessi made no attempt to disguise himself, he was intolerant of intrusion. Often, people would stare at him, or approach our table, and say, "Excuse me, but aren't you Plessi Toussaint, the author?"

Most often, Plessi wouldn't even look up. Or if he did, he might blow smoke in their faces, or drop ashes on their shoes. "Who?" he would say.

"Plessi Toussaint, the author. He wrote *Condamné, Magnéto, Crédillon.*"

"Never heard of him."

"Well, you could pass for his twin. Although come to think of it, what would such a renowned writer of pulp fiction be doing here at this time of year? He's probably in Paris, digging up dirt on the chief of police."

I once said to Plessi, "Why be famous if you don't want people to recognize you? If it was me, I'd be thrilled. I've struggled for years to be known, and I'm still obscure. No one ever comes up to me in a restaurant and asks for my autograph. Certainly not in places like St-Tropez."

He thought this over. "Which is why I tolerate you, mon gars. If you were famous, and your ego as big as mine, we would be incompatible. I would have nothing to do with you. As it is, you're stupid, but no threat. What's more, you don't bore me. You don't ask for advice. You sit all day in your dusty room, looking out the window, waiting for—how do you call it?—a bolt from the blue. When that fails, you walk round town like a homeless dog, bored to tears, looking for someone to talk to. God knows what you do at night when I'm

working. Maybe you sleep. Maybe you hide in the park, waiting to pounce on unsuspecting girls. Or unsuspecting boys.
You refuse to let me make you an appointment with Yvette
Chanteloup, so maybe you pass the time playing with yourself. But at least you don't bother me. You don't knock on my
door and demand to know the secret for writing best sellers.
If you did, I would tell you to fuck off."

To be truthful, I found his lofty, supercilious tone annoy-
ing. "I'm sure you would, Monsieur Toussaint. But still, being
recognized must be flattering. Unless of course you're
ashamed of yourself."

He snorted, stuck out his tongue. "I assure you, my stupid young friend, I'm not ashamed of myself. Au contraire.
But if I admitted to these assholes who I am, they would bury
me in worthless manuscripts, force their stupid ideas on me.
They would tell me what my next book should be about. They
would cling like leeches, buy me drinks, invite me to orgies."

"But that sounds wonderful! I thought that was the
whole idea."

He banged down his wine glass and stood up, breathing
fire. "Nom de Dieu, you're even stupider than I thought! I
may disown you yet, mon gars. You're a half-wit. There's a
time and a place for those thing, but not while one is working. If one lose the thread, it may be lost forever. *Merde!* All I
care is that people buy my books. I don't want them to talk
to me. I don't want their stupid ideas. I have enough of my
own. I don't even want my editor, or my agent, Henri Barrage, to talk to me. I want them to shut their mouths!"

"Then you should wear ear plugs, Monsieur Toussaint.
Grow a beard. Buy a wig. Put on sunglasses."

"What?" he shouted, making Marius jump, drawing
everyone's attention. "And lose my identity? Never!"

I thought he might be going to order me away, but he
didn't. He sat down, finally, signalled Marius for another
carafe of wine, helped himself to one of my cigarettes. I could
be wrong, but I thought he was as close to smiling as I'd yet
seen him. "Mon gars," he said, tapping me on the hand, "isn't

it ironic that I would give anything, me, to have again some of the obscurity you say you are trying to escape? If only we could trade places." His smile faded and he looked very serious. "I mean it. I remember the joy of those difficult days, when I was sincere and honest, when my friends were not jealous. I could walk down boulevard St-Michel in Paris under the chestnut trees and enjoy myself. I could pass the day at Luxembourg Gardens. I could invite *littérateurs* to my apartment on rue de Torbigo and discuss books. I could sit at Brasserie Lipp or Les Deux Magots on a spring afternoon and drink vermouth with pretty women. Now, I must always be on guard against people who see themselves in my books. I have paranoid enemies, mon gars. My money escapes me, but my enemies remain. True, there are still those who envy me, but there are also those who hate my gut. Is that how you say it in English? Hate my gut?"

"Hate my guts."

"Oui, hate my guts. There are those who hate my guts. Who imagine themselves slandered, or at least painted too accurately. Even when I change the names. Did you ever read the works of Henry Miller or Truman Capote? I am compared to them. They say that in the end, people hated their guts too. Threw stones at them, as well as lawsuits. I am also compared to your Michael Ondaatje, and to that mad Columbian, Gabriel Marquez. Do they hate him also?"

"It's possible," I said. "I know they hate Norman Mailer."

"Ah, the great Norman Mailer! I once met him at an international writers' conference in Toronto. We read to huge crowds down at the water. I tried to talk to him, but like everyone else, we were both very drunk. All we could do was grunt like pigs at each other. He hadn't read my books, I hadn't read his. At the time, he was in big trouble because of some convict. He once stabbed his wife, you know. No wonder people hate his guts. If I had a wife, I might stab her too. It's a good thing I never married. Like André Gide, I almost married my cousin. Her name was Gabrielle. But her parents, my aunt and uncle, annulled it, which was a good thing. Do you believe me?"

"Of course I believe you. Shouldn't I?"

"No, you shouldn't. I made it all up. I have no cousin Gabrielle. You're *facile à duper*, mon gars. Easily duped. A serious writer is not easily duped."

One evening in November a pair of Irish ladies came into Le Gorille and sat down at the table next to ours. They were well dressed, respectable-looking women, one tall, the other short, and their lilting Irish accents, as they ordered onion soup and coquilles St-Jacques, were pleasing to the ear. As often happened, they were soon staring at Plessi. Which I thought remarkable, because although his books are available in several languages, and Ireland is a very literary country, these two women looked more like the George Bernard Shaw type. Plessi was aware of their scrutiny too, but for once, didn't seem to mind. In fact, he raised his wine glass to them, nodded in their direction.

"You'll forgive me, sir," the taller lady said, returning his salute with her own wine glass, "but you bear an uncanny likeness to that writer of shocking books, Plessi Toussaint. You could be mistaken for him, you could indeed."

To my surprise, Plessi said, "Well, I should hope so, madame. You're very astute. You have sharp eyes. Would you care to come and join us? Like you, my friend and I are only at our soup course."

Which is how, that November evening in St-Tropez, we met Dora Dundalk and Polly Roscommon, pensioners from the Emerald Isle. Plessi, intrigued, said later he viewed them as potential characters in a story. Polly, a widow since 1957, was tall and thin. She had greying hair, furtive eyes, wore bifocals. Her friend and travelling companion, Dora Dundalk, a spinster, was a shorter, less noticeable woman. She had bobbed brown hair and a perpetual, though at times vacant, smile.

The interesting thing about Dora and Polly was that though they differed in appearance, they could have been sisters. They finished each other's sentences, seemed able to communicate telepathically. They'd been acquainted since childhood, had gone to school together at Sligo. Later, they'd both become teachers, though Polly had briefly given up the profession in 1956 to get married and move east to Athlone. She admitted being unhappy, living so far from the sea and having to sleep with a sweaty man. Dora had been maid of honour at her wedding, which took place in Ballyshannon, and then had been her main support when Polly's husband, a roofer named Comyn, had fallen from the peak of the city hall in Galway and died of his injuries. After a summer of mourning, Polly had returned to the classroom, at an elementary school in Bundoran, where she taught primary grades for the next thirty-five years.

When Plessi asked what had brought them to St-Tropez in late autumn, Polly said, "Sure, at this time of year, when the crowds diminish, we always take a train trip on the continent. Travel is an Irish obsession, it is. We're a nation of wanderers, all the way back to Saint Brendan in his skin boat. He discovered France, you know. He took shamrocks with him for good luck when he visited the New World. He sailed with Ulysses on the Mediterranean. I dare say he knew Saint Tropes, the monk this place is named after, who was beheaded by Nero for being a Christian believer, as was Saint Brendan himself."

"Speaking of saints," Dora said, "we've been to St-Malo, St-Benoit, St-Germain-en-Laye, St-Jean-de-Luz, St-Lô, St-Rémy and St-Pol-de-Léon. It's a thing we have about saints. It's why we've come to St-Tropez. We only go to saintly places. Sure, and the only time we didn't was the year our friend Sheena was on trial for the killing of her wee baby, poor thing, when all along we knew it was her husband Seamus that did it, and ran off to Belfast, coward that he is, to join the IRA. May the devil take him."

Polly signalled Marius for another bottle of Côtes du Rhône. "And you yourself, Plessi Toussaint, whose skill with a scandalous tale I rank next to our native son, James Joyce, what brings you to St-Tropez at this dismal season?"

"I'm working on a book," Plessi said.

Polly put down her fork. "Are you now? And what might it be about, if a person could be so bold?"

I was sure Plessi would tell her to mind her own business, that it was bad luck to discuss a work in progress, but he fooled me. "It's about a closet transvestite, Pierre Herbois, presently crown prosecutor of Paris. His grand'mère was the novelist, Sidonie Colette, who lived here in St-Tropez before the war and raised silkworms. On the side of his papa, he's descended from Buisson Pampellone, inventor of the bidet."

Dora put down her fork too, filled everyone's wine glass, without waiting for Marius. "Faith, now," she said. "Imagine that. Descended from the inventor of the bidet. Better, I suppose, than from the inventor of that other French device, the guillotine."

"We don't have bidets in Ireland," Polly said to no one in particular. "We've seen them in various hotels. We have one here in our bathroom at Les Lauriers, as a matter of fact. I've never really understood its purpose."

This was met with silence. Both women looked at me, as though expecting to be enlightened. But as I'd said nothing thus far, I felt no compulsion to open my mouth now.

Plessi sat back, gulped his wine, lit a pungent Gauloise. "Monsieur Pampellone, unless I'm mistaken, intend the bidet for use after sex."

This produced further silence, although I noticed people at other tables eavesdropping.

"Really?" Dora said. "How interesting. I would have thought that the man's name would be Monsieur Bidet."

I could hear people around us snickering. Even Marius had a smile on his face.

"No," Plessi said, "his name is Buisson Pampellone. Le bidet is also a small horse. A pony. One sit on the bidet as one sit on the small horse. Especially women."

Dora was visibly impressed. "Fancy that. Something else we have at Les Lauriers is mirrors in the bedroom. I could never see the need for so many mirrors in the bedroom. Did your Monsieur Pampellone invent those too?"

"Oui, madame, he did. But for use during sex, not after. They say he have a Basque mistress, who enjoy watching the action, especially when she entertain Monsieur Pampellone's brother Henri, the Minister of Health."

"And that's what your book is about?"

"Ah, non, madame. My book is about le président, Jacques Chirac, and his prime minister, Alain Juppé, and about the brothels of Paris, where they have bidets on the floor and mirrors on the ceiling."

But he had underestimated Polly Roscommon, who, despite the wine she'd consumed, remembered what he'd said earlier. "I thought you told us your book was about a transvestite crown prosecutor named Herbois."

Plessi was only momentarily flummoxed. "Did I, madame? Well, it's true. My book is about all three, Chirac, Juppé and Herbois, the nephew of Edith Piaf. The mayor of Paris, Monsieur Douste-Blazy, is also involved. Plus a great many Parisian harlots. I may have to go into exile."

Dora clapped her hands, signalled Marius for yet another bottle of wine. "You could always come to Ireland, Monsieur Toussaint. We could hide you in Dublin, where our friend Sheena, that never killed her baby, lives. We could put you up at the Gresham Hotel and let you drink the dark Guinness all day long."

Polly was enthused too. "And erect a statue of you beside Brendan Behan in O'Connell Street. Sure, wouldn't that be grand, with yourself as important a personage as Jonathan Swift."

But Dora, who had consumed as much wine as anyone, was suddenly off on a different tack. "I'm sad to say, the only useful things the Irish have invented are the condom and the potato."

Polly grimaced, apparently dubious. "The condom, my dear? I hardly think so. Surely it was the French. Isn't that why it's called a French letter?"

"It was invented by Dr. Condom, an Irish physician, in 1760. Out of a sheep's intestine. The Catholics in Northern Ireland call it Beelzebub's rubber. I don't know where it got the name French letter. Perhaps Monsieur Toussaint knows."

But Plessi, for all his bluster and wine capacity, had grown strangely silent. It was as though, in the realm of tall tales, he'd met his match. Or he may simply have been enthralled. Or fatigued. If he knew why condoms were called French letters, he wasn't saying. All he did was shake his head. I guessed he might have been back with Saint Brendan, sailing the Mediterranean, meeting Ulysses and the headless Saint Tropes.

Curiously, everyone looked at me. All three pairs of eyes appeared blurred, out of focus. Unable to recall the question, I felt an uncontrollable urge to giggle. "Potatoes," I said, "came from South America. I believe they were first cultivated by the Indians."

But Polly disagreed. "You're thinking of the sweet potato, I'm afraid. If you aspire to be a clever writer like Monsieur Toussaint, you must verify your facts. The white potato was, and is, native to Ireland. Of that, you may be sure. Otherwise, why would we have had the great potato famine in 1846?"

The evening ended, as I recall, amid smoke and empty wine bottles, with Dora and Polly asking Plessi if he'd favour them with a reading.

"I don't give readings," he said thickly.

"Is it beneath your dignity?" Polly asked.

"I have no dignity, madame."

"James Joyce gave readings. So did Sean O'Casey. So did Samuel Beckett, in both English and French. He taught school in Paris, you know. And in Cork, as well. Dora and I once went to hear him read *Waiting for Godot* in Dublin. It was a marvelous thing, it was, at Kitty O'Shea's pub on Canal Street. They took a silver collection."

"I don't give readings."

"Is it that you're afraid?"

"I don't give readings in bars or restaurants. You'd have to come to my apartment. But only one of you. I couldn't read to both of you at the same time."

I remember being foggily amused by this, even though I had no idea what Plessi was up to. I couldn't imagine him having designs on either woman. Surely he wasn't that warped. It might have been his way of turning the tide, of regaining control. I knew of no one who'd ever been invited to his apartment at Filles du Soleil, for readings or anything else. Not even Yvette Chanteloup, from Crêperie Bretonne. So this was either a great honour or a ruse. People at other tables were listening intently now, and I realized that Plessi and the Irish ladies were talking very loudly. Marius stood off to one side, pretending to be disinterested.

"It would have to be the two of us," Polly said. "Or not at all."

"Is it that you're afraid?" Plessi said gleefully, almost shouting. "Come up to my apartment, one at a time, and see my bidet. I'll give you a reading you won't soon forget."

"No," Dora said, shouting right back at him. "It's that we don't know if you're really who you say you are. We've learned in our travels to be wary of Frenchmen, Turks and Italians. You could be an impostor. You've told some scary stories here this evening. For all we know, you could be a sex fiend, trying to lure us to our doom!"

"Don't flatter yourself, madame. I'm Plessi Toussaint, the author."

"Well, so you say. But I think Plessi Toussaint is a younger man. And taller. And I don't think Plessi Toussaint would wear such a silly hat."

"I'm Plessi Toussaint, madame! I write books."

"So you keep saying. Which makes me wonder if you really are. You seem insecure."

And that's when I think Plessi knew he'd been bested. Polly and Dora were too much for him. They'd beaten him at his own game. The wine had all been drunk, the cigarettes all smoked. What remained were fish bones and bread crumbs. Around the room, there was a smattering of applause, as though the patrons of Le Gorille had been treated to a skit, a comedy in one act.

I suppose I should have felt sorry for Plessi, should have come to his rescue. But for some strange reason, I didn't.

St-Tropez Lighthouse

Chapter Three

I must admit, I wasn't looking forward to Christmas. As has been my lot in life, I was far from home and nearly friendless. Other than Plessi, I'd succeeded in making no intimate acquaintances. True, had it not been for his easy accessibility, and having drinks with him every day, I might have tried harder. Oddly enough, his was the only social contact I seemed to need. He was such a complex, interesting person, a man of so many moods and biases, that he held my attention. I confess I was rather intimidated by him though, and because of that, was afraid to tackle any serious writing. At least, that was my excuse.

He was right about one thing—I did spend much of my time wandering. I watched children hurrying to and from school. I watched boys on bicycles, pursued by dogs, racing through Place des Lices and being yelled at by elderly pétanque players. I spent a morning in the cemetery of Notre Dame de l'Esterel, on rue des Blancs Manteaux, looking at tombstones. I watched old women tending flower boxes on their balconies. I watched street sweepers and refuse collectors. I watched fishermen coming ashore with their catches for the market on quai Jean-Jaurès. Shipwrights worked on millionaire's yachts in the harbour, preparing them for next season. On cloudless days, old men sat on benches facing the sea, the sun warming their faces. Behind them, the same sun bronzed the picturesque old buildings along quai Suffren, hiding their cracks and blemishes. Even my rooming house, Filles du Soleil, looked presentable.

One beautiful December morning, I went into the book shop on the ground floor of Filles du Soleil, which also sells art supplies, and bought a sketch pad and fifty wax crayons. The first thing I drew was the *Citadelle*—that ruined 16th-century stone fortress on the breakwater, with gulls perched across its roof. I sat by the sea wall for two hours, mellow from breakfast grogs, pretending to be an artist. Then I sketched the St-Tropez lighthouse, with a rainbow over it, and after that the old brick Customs building, at the end of its crumbling pier, guarded by cormorants. As the light changed and intensified, I began to see why Matisse and his Impressionist cohorts had come here to paint in the 1890s. While my pictures were not good enough to show anyone, least of all Plessi, they added to my contentment, made me feel in tune with my surroundings. Most mornings, after two rum grogs and a half dozen Gauloises, I could convince myself I was happy. Only when Plessi asked me if I'd started my novel yet, and if not, why not? did I feel a twinge of conscience.

He'd said he might be going to Paris in mid-December, even though his publisher, Gallimard, and his agent, Henri Barrage, had advised against it. They told him he should stay where he was, out of harm's way, with his nose to the grindstone, and not risk missing his Easter deadline.

"They are inhuman slave drivers," he said one evening at supper, as we dined by candlelight at Le Gorille, hovered over by a new waiter, Baptiste, while Marius was on vacation in Grenoble.

"Perhaps they know you too well," I said. "Or else they have your best interests at heart."

"Whatever they have at heart, mon gars, it is not my best interests. True, I sometimes get side-tracked and miss deadlines, but always for a reason, such as delirium tremens. That's what happens when one sobers up too fast. *La folie d'ivresse.* And what does it matter whether a book appears in summer or in winter? All they think of is their profit. The only worse parasite than a publisher, nom de Dieu, is an agent, and the only worse parasite than an agent is a pedophile priest."

Contrary to their promises, my friends Dinard and Pascaline sent not one postcard. They might as well have dropped off the face of the earth. I suspected they'd found a commune with a good supply of hashish. The two Irish ladies, on the other hand, Dora and Polly, who hadn't promised anything, wrote to Plessi from St-Julien, near Geneva, and from St-Claude, in the Jura mountains. They said they'd seen his books in many book stores, translated into German and Italian, but had come to the conclusion that the bidet was losing its European popularity. In Americanized hotels, such as the Sheraton and the Marriott, where the bidet was missing, the managers considered it old fashioned. Which was unfortunate, just when they themselves had finally figured out how to use it, how to "ride the small horse." Changes in technology, they said, for two unsophisticated Irish ladies, were hard to keep up with and not always beneficial. Oh, and on the train to St-Jean de Maurienne, close to the Swiss border, they'd had dinner in the dining car with a Monsieur Pouilleuse, who said he was a distant cousin of Jacques Chirac. He expressed great interest in Plessi's forthcoming book, concerning the president's sordid dalliances. He said he intended to buy a dozen copies of it for his family. Wasn't the world a small place?

Two weeks before Christmas, a new tenant moved into the apartment next to mine at Filles du Soleil. He was an older man, perhaps in his sixties, and the first time I saw him, sitting alone at Le Gorille, he was reading *L'Express* and drinking a rum grog. It seemed to be the drink of choice at St-Tropez, at least on winter afternoons.

He was wearing a beige trench coat and smoking a cigarette. The first thing you noticed about him was his bushy white eyebrows. Because he had a receding hairline, his eyebrows really stood out. The rest of his hair was white too, combed straight back, which somehow emphasized his sunken cheeks and creased face. I would have pegged him as a spy, or a jaded foreign correspondent, who sends back dispatches from around the world and spends too much in bars.

But I was wrong. His name was Honoré Velmandois and he was a former professor of English at the Sorbonne. When I sat down across from him and asked him in French if there were anything new or startling in his newspaper, he was not overly friendly.

"From your accent and impertinence," he said, "I'd judge you were American."

"Close," I said, captivated by his low, melodious, professor's voice and precise way of talking. "Canadian."

"And why would a Canadian find himself in St-Tropez at this time of year? Shouldn't you be home skiing or chasing polar bears across the tundra?"

"I'm trying to write a book. From your own accent, I'd say you've spent time at Oxford or Cambridge."

"I have a degree in English literature from Leeds. Also one from Nottingham. What kind of book?"

"A novel. A sequel to my recent *Crown of Wild Olives*."

He gave me a blank look. "And that's what you do for a living? Write novels?"

"It's not much of a living."

We sat in silence then, watching two old men beside us playing backgammon. They shook the dice hard, but played silently, sipping cloudy glasses of pastis. I offered Honoré a cigarette, but when he saw they were Gauloises, he declined and went back to his newspaper. I caught Baptiste's eye, signalled for two rum grogs, and when he brought them, I paid for both. I couldn't tell if Honoré was surprised or annoyed. Certainly not grateful.

"That wasn't necessary."

"No, it wasn't. But I needed one and yours is nearly finished. Do you know Plessi Toussaint? He recommends these highly, as an aid to digestion."

"I've never met Monsieur Toussaint, but I've read his books. He's won the Prix Médici several times."

"He's here in St-Tropez too."

"Yes, I was aware of that."

"He lives where I do, at Filles du Soleil."

"I've rented a Filles du Soleil apartment as well. I stayed there once, a long time ago, the year my wife and I separated. It wasn't nearly so—how do you say... rundown? I was drunk for three days. I don't remember much."

"But you've read Plessi Toussaint's books?"

"Of course. Who hasn't? He's our national treasure. Our gossip columnist. Every Parisian has read his books. He lives in a bohemian apartment in the heart of Paris, you know, on rue Vaugirard, near St-Sulpice cathedral. It's a quarter I know well. I'm surprised he's not there now."

"I believe his life's been threatened."

"Little wonder. Is he your friend?"

"We eat breakfast together. Sometimes supper. We drink rum grogs, discuss writing. He works all night, sleeps during the day."

"I was aware of that. And you?"

"I keep normal hours. I sleep at night."

"As God intended. Are you married?"

"No."

"Are you gay?"

"No."

"Good. I was hoping you weren't. The way you sat down uninvited and started a conversation, I wondered. I've been approached before. As a matter of fact, everywhere I go, I'm approached. At my age, it can get tiresome. Is Plessi Toussaint?"

"Gay? Definitely not."

"I didn't think so. That would ruin his image."

"He visits a girl quite regularly at Crêperie Bretonne, down the street. Her name is Yvette Chanteloup. She knows what he likes."

We'd both finished our grogs, and when Baptiste came by, Honoré ordered two more. The sun was shining. The afternoon was beginning to take on a soft, golden glow. A feeling of well-being crept over me. Even the sea gulls' raucous cries seemed fitting, as did the rumble of boat engines out in the harbour. I asked Honoré how long he planned to stay at Filles du Soleil.

"I've decided to spend Christmas. Paris is cold and damp this year. There are demonstrations in the streets every weekend. Riots. Protests. Students marching against globalization, global warming, global terrorism. Paris is full of immigrants. At the moment, immigrants outnumber tourists. There's a

walk. Not without Baptiste's aid. Honoré must have been in better shape, because he introduced himself to Plessi, told him how much he enjoyed his books, congratulated him on winning the Prix Médici. I heard him say that as a professor of English at the Sorbonne, he felt qualified to pass judgement, and his judgement was that Plessi was a good writer, a master of the modern French novel, no matter what certain of his critics thought. In his opinion, Plessi was better even than Eugène Bordet or Ambroisie Pacaud. Anyone published by Gallimard deserved acclaim, because Gallimard did not publish second-rate authors.

Though Plessi had a long way to go to catch up, he gave it his best effort. He downed several rum grogs quickly and soon he and Honoré both had flushed faces and slurred speech. I'm ashamed to say, I fell by the wayside, and while they got acquainted and made each other laugh, I sat there, more or less stupified. When they thought I wasn't listening, they spoke in French. When I made inarticulate sounds that passed for conversation, they reverted to English. I remember being pleased that they seemed to like each other. By the time Baptiste brought us our prawns and oysters and a chilled bottle of Sancerre, they were calling each other "tu" and carrying on like old friends. It was heart-warming. Two men, meeting for the first time, behaving like buddies. Where, I wondered, was the usual French reserve, the innate suspicion of strangers?

The last thing I remember is being helped across the street by Baptiste whose shift was over and who volunteered to assist me up the stairs of Filles du Soleil to my room. When I left, Plessi Toussaint and Honoré Velmandois, true champion literary men, one practical, the other theoretical, were still at Le Gorille, telling jokes, feasting on snails and mussels and sharing yet another bottle of chilled Sancerre. As I fell into my spinning bed, I was happy to have had a small part in bringing them together. The bad news? Plessi got no writing done that night. The good news? Persuasive Honoré talked him out of going to Paris for Christmas.

I became aware of their plans a night or two later, when the three of us were dining at Le Gorille. Plessi, it seems, since he wasn't going to Paris, had expressed a desire to visit the coastal village of Agay, fifty kilometres east of St-Tropez, between Cap Dramont and Pointe du Cap Rouge. His reason? A literary friend of his, Lise Escarène, author of moderately successful novels and a biography or two, had invited him to spend a few days at her villa. Since she was not a religious person, Christmas seemed as good a time as any. The idea of going to Agay pleased Honoré too, because it was the birthplace of a famous French aviator he'd admired all his life—Antoine de St-Exupéry. Growing up, he'd hoped to become a pilot, but had lacked the necessary skills. So he'd had to be content with reading about St-Exupéry's adventures in Patagonia between the wars, establishing airmail routes through the Andes. To see his hero's birthplace, he said, would please him enormously, especially as the St-Exupéry family château had been turned into a museum. He'd also heard that you could visit Antoine's grave in the Agay cemetery, and view the spot nearby where he'd been shot down by the Germans in 1944.

As it turned out, Plessi Toussaint had an interest in St-Exupéry too. Not through aviation or Antoine's writings, but because his brilliant biographer, a scholarly woman named Stacey Schiff, was a friend of Plessi's. She'd also written a biography of Vladimir Nabokov's wife, Véra, and Plessi had helped her research this fascinating woman at the Bibliothèque Nationale in Paris during the winter of 1998.

And so it was decided that an expedition would be mounted to Lise Escarène's villa at Agay. A basket of Provençal wine and other delicacies would be taken to her. At first, I thought that Plessi and Honoré planned to go without me. But they didn't. I expected they'd ride the train to Cannes and catch a bus from there. But they didn't. Their desire was to rent a car and go in style. For that, of course, they needed a driver. Unfortunately, Honoré had no license. Neither had Plessi. I found this hard to believe, until Honoré explained that living in Paris, he'd relied on taxis and the métro. In his younger day, he'd used a bicycle. During the latter half of his teaching career, he'd lived on rue des Carmes, a stone's throw from the Sorbonne, and had walked to work. A car in Paris, for anyone but a dare-devil or tank commander, was a danger and a liability. His wife had owned one, a Deux Chevaux convertible, but she was a maniac, *une folle furieuse*, behind the wheel, and he had seldom ridden in it. When he went away to Versailles or Fontainebleau on weekends, he'd always taken the train.

With Plessi, the story was slightly different. He too had once owned a Deux Chevaux convertible, but had wrecked it and lost his license driving home drunk one night from Rambouillet. Though he wasn't hurt, the gendarmes on the scene had been inflexible, had chastised him and put him in jail.

And so the agreement was that if I would drive them to Lise Escarène's villa at Agay, and bring them safely back, they would cover all expenses. The two of them could easily afford it. I said I'd be happy to assume the role of chauffeur and valet, but not of nursemaid. We sealed the bargain with a toast of Cointreau.

Next day after breakfast the three of us went to the Europcar rental agency on rue Sibilli. The sun was out and it was a fine December morning. A pétanque tournament was in progress under the plane trees at place Carnot. Six whiskery old men were silently throwing brass balls, observed by a hundred spectators. Overhead, magpies kept up a crackling commentary. The pale, uniformed girl behind the Europcar counter, whose name was Danielle, gave us a boxy white Peugeot sedan, which, while neither stylish nor brand new, suited us. Plessi asked her if she'd like to come along for the ride, and when she demurred, he told her she was the second person that day to turn him down. The first, it transpired, had been Yvette Chanteloup at Crêperie Bretonne. He said that even had Yvette been able to take time off from the pancake shop, her off-premises fee was, in his words, astronomically prohibitive. "Still, she would have been good company, mon gars," he said to me. "A pleasant distraction."

That evening at Le Gorille, on the eve of our departure, Honoré produced a road map and we plotted our course. A brief stop would be made at Port Grimaud, to see canals and bridges, followed by a detour to the limestone cliffs at Ramatuelle, for a view of medieval streets and a Romanesque church. Then east to Ste-Maxime, where Plessi had once spent July on the beach with a girl named Estelle. "What a coincidence," Honoré said. "After my wife left for Polynesia, I had an affair with a student in one of my classes whose name was Estelle. She told me she was a virgin, but I don't think she was. Unfortunately, she asked her father for advice, and I was reprimanded."

From Ste-Maxime, we would push on through Roman vineyards and porphry outcroppings to Fréjus, where Julius Caesar lived two thousand years ago, and where there is a 10th-century cathedral. We might or might not pause at the seaside town of St-Raphael, where the liberation of the Riviera by Allied forces began in August of 1944. Our final stop would be at Agay, in front of Lise Escarène's villa, overlooking the deep cove where traders from ancient Greece once anchored their galleys.

"You see, mon gars," Plessi said to me, "besides conducting the Peugeot, you will also have a history lesson. In your country, you have no history. First Indians, then the French and English, but no excitement. No Greeks. No Romans. No Moors. Here, you will learn things. And if that has no appeal, you will at least meet Lise Escarène."

"Will she be expecting us?"

"Don't be stupid, mon gars. Old friends prefer to be surprised. Otherwise, preparation is required."

Though we planned an early start next morning, we stayed up late that night at Le Gorille, eating cheese tarts and drinking chilled Meursault. At midnight, Baptiste brought us onion soup and croque-monsieur sandwiches, which no one remembered ordering. Long after we should have been in our respective beds at Filles du Soleil, Plessi and Honoré began a wine-fuelled debate as to who was the best English novelist, living or dead. Though it was Honoré's field of expertise, Plessi had definite opinions. People at nearby tables had opinions too. Paper serviettes were torn up and used as ballots. Honoré appointed himself returning officer, took out his pen and began recording votes. There was so much banter, however, that dawn was breaking before he finished compiling a list of favourites. Ernest Hemingway and Lawrence Durrell tied for first place. William Faulkner was dead last. In between were Malcolm Lowry, John Updike, Thornton Wilder and Herman Wouk. That so much was known about English authors amazed me. Consensus was that among French novelists, Marcel Proust was too far out in front to warrant further argument. But if pushed for a runner-up, the electorate would be torn between Plessi Toussaint and Albert Camus. To acknowledge this accolade, Plessi rose, bowed, raised his glass, then toppled over sideways and had to be helped back into his chair. He said he was honoured to be mentioned in the same breath as Proust and Camus, knew he didn't merit it, and that Simone de Beauvoir deserved mention too. His magnanimity was praised, a toast drunk, an empty Meursault bottle presented as a trophy.

The sun was about to rise when Honoré suggested that we postpone our departure for Agay till the afternoon, or possibly the next day. It seemed like a good idea. Arm in arm, singing snatches of *La Marseillaise*, we weaved our unsteady way home to Filles du Soleil.

La Marine, St-Tropez

Chapter Four

As Plessi said on Christmas Eve, when we were sitting indoors at Le Gorille, drinking martinis, with no one for company but the two waiters, Baptiste and Marius—it's a good thing we weren't halfway to Lise Escarène's house when Honoré had his heart attack. It was also a good thing we hadn't told Lise to expect us, because we never got there.

The afternoon we were to leave, Honoré said he didn't feel well. Truthfully, none of us felt well. After staying up all night at Le Gorille, drinking and eating and discussing novelists, we all had hangovers. Which was not out of the ordinary. But at lunch, Honoré, who could swallow nothing, said he felt weak and disoriented. All morning, he'd suffered dizzy spells. When the concierge of Filles du Soleil, Monsieur Nemours, carrying out his weekly inspection, had asked Honoré why he was still in bed, why he was pale and perspiring, Honoré had said he thought he might need a doctor. To which the concierge replied, "What you need, monsieur, is to stay away from Plessi Toussaint and Le Gorille."

And so once again we postponed our departure for Agay, until such time as Honoré felt better. While I patrolled the waterfront, or sat by myself at La Marine, Plessi returned to his Chirac book, attacking it with renewed vigour, as though it were an adversary, who, if not subdued, might harm him.

That evening, Honoré tried to get out of bed and join us at Le Gorille for supper, but couldn't. By then, his throat had constricted and he was seeing double. Plessi took him a glass of water, helped him sit up and drink it. He said, "You have a virus, my friend. A fever. Here are some aspirin."

But Plessi's faith in aspirin was naive. At midnight, when he looked in on Honoré, he found him on the floor, hunched over, unable to speak. So Plessi went and woke Monsieur Nemours, told him to summon an ambulance. Then he came and woke me, in case I was needed. When the ambulance arrived, two young paramedics, a boy and a girl, ran upstairs with Plessi, put Honoré on a stretcher, carried him down to the street. He was groaning, sweating, had his hands clasped over his chest. I heard the paramedics calling the hospital on their radio, telling them to prepare for the arrival of a *crise cardiaque*. Plessi wanted to board the ambulance too, but they wouldn't let him. They placed an oxygen mask over Honoré's face, injected something into his arm, then drove off with their lights flashing and their siren howling. Down those dark streets, the noise was deafening, alarming, until it faded away to nothing.

Since the white Peugeot was sitting there, in front of Filles du Soleil, Plessi and I got in it and drove to the St-Tropez clinic on rue Gassin. We found the ambulance parked at the *Entrée d'Urgences*, empty, but with its lights still flashing. I followed Plessi inside, was aware of nurses in blue uniforms scurrying about, two doctors with stethoscopes around their necks, anxious voices behind a green curtain. Seeing us standing there, a nurse approached, asked if we were relatives of the heart attack victim. We said we were only friends, not relatives, and she led us over to a computer and began typing in our answers to her questions. I remember thinking how calm everyone seemed, except for those behind the green curtain. I wondered if Honoré were already dead. Besides the hospital sounds, I remember the hospital smells, and the long corridor, with all its signs in French. I remember thinking to myself that this wasn't fair. That Honoré hadn't deserved this. Though I scarcely knew him, I felt sorry for him, stricken at the festive season, far from home, without warning. He was a nice man, an intelligent, interesting man, and this was not fair.

Plessi and I stayed at the clinic until four o'clock in the morning, smoking Gauloises, not speaking. Twice, the same nurse gave us coffee and told us we might as well go home. Finally, she said that Monsieur Velmandois was stable, sedated, out of immediate danger, but unable to receive visitors. The doctors had succeeded in normalizing his *tension artérielle* and regulating his heartbeat. His blood had been thinned, his arteries dilated. Oxygen was once again coursing to his organs. Fortunately, he did not appear to have suffered *un coup cérébral,* but it was perhaps too early to tell. Did we know whether Monsieur Velmandois had a history of *apoplexie*? No, we didn't. Did he have a wife somewhere? Grown children? Someone who should be notified? What was his address in Paris? Could we provide the hospital with his *carte d'identité,* his social security number, his medical registration? We said we'd try, but made no promises. Was Monsieur Velmandois a heavy smoker? A heavy drinker? Comme tout le monde, mademoiselle. Like all of us. No better, no worse. He was, above all, a good man, a good friend.

At four a.m. I drove us back to Filles du Soleil in the white Peugeot. There were tendrils of mist in the streets, cats prowling. Out on the breakwall, the St-Tropez lighthouse winked, signalling non-existent ships. The breeze off the Mediterranean was gentle, richly scented, blowing across the sea from Africa. I thought Plessi might have invited me to his apartment for a nightcap, but he didn't. He said, "I suppose you plan to sleep now, mon gars?"

"Eventually. And you?"

"Back to work on my book. I feel energized. I think I can put in three or four good hours. I have some difficult dialogue to get through, but I think now I can do it. Later, I'll go and tell my troubles to Yvette at Crêperie Bretonne."

"You amaze me. You truly amaze me."

"This is not a hobby of stamps, mon ami. This is my life's work. Tonight, in the midst of turmoil, I receive a valuable flash of inspiration. If you are a serious writer, you know what I mean."

As he turned to climb the stairs, he said, "Someday, with or without Monsieur Velmandois, we will pay our visit to my colleague, Lise Escarène. I think you would like her."

Honoré Velmandois was in the St-Tropez clinic over Christmas. Plessi and I visited him every day, sometimes together, sometimes separately. Plessi told him that when he was transferred to Paris, the two of them could co-habit his apartment on rue Vaugirard, near St-Sulpice cathedral. Honoré thanked him, said that when the time came, he'd be glad of a place to stay. To me, the offer sounded sincere, if impractical, and I was struck by Plessi's generosity.

Since we didn't need the white Peugeot, we returned it to Danielle at the Europcar agency on rue Sibilli. Plessi asked her if she had a fiancé, and when she said no, not at the moment, he proposed that she come and visit him at Filles du Soleil and "cause joy to the soul of a jaded author whose every orgasm might be his last."

At first, Honoré was in a darkened room by himself, attached to a beeping monitor, with electrodes on his chest. A nurse came in every half hour, took his blood pressure, listened to his pulse, gave him tablets to swallow. He was allowed no excitement, no cigarettes, only brief visits. Then he was moved into a room with a white-bearded, skeletal old man, who lay on his back with his mouth open, staring at the ceiling. Now and again he groaned, muttered something about scorpions in the toilet. As soon as Honoré's electrodes were removed, he began taking short walks as far as the sun room at the end of the corridor. His face began to lose its pallor. He ate his meals sitting up. Someone cut his hair. The nurses said he was making progress, would soon be transported by ambulance to St-Victor coronary centre in Marseille, where, depending on circumstances, an operation might be performed on his arteries. From Marseille, he would be transferred to the Frémicourt rehabilitation facility in Paris. But he must never smoke cigarettes again, or drink too much wine. He must be careful with his diet. As well, he must sleep ten hours a day, avoid anger and violence, take the necessary number of prescribed pills.

Before Honoré went to Marseille, Plessi Toussaint and I spent a lot of time at Le Gorille, eating, drinking, talking to Marius and Baptiste. Christmas Eve, and again Christmas Day, Plessi visited Yvette Chanteloup at Crêperie Bretonne. He asked me to go with him, and I almost did, but the prospect of sharing Yvette did not appeal to me. Or maybe it was Yvette who did not appeal to me. At least not when I was sober. Instead, Christmas Day, I walked two kilometres to the St-Tropez clinic on rue Gassin and watched television with Honoré in the sun room. He said he'd decided that as soon as his strength returned, in six months or so, he planned to fly to Tahiti and look for his adopted daughters. After all these years, they wouldn't know him, but so what? He wasn't their real father anyway. Perhaps by now he had grandchildren. While in Tahiti, he might visit his ex-wife's grave, if he could find it, and if her second husband didn't mind. He might even discover what tropical disease she'd died of. Or did I think these impulses foolish, brought on by his medication? He suspected that might be the case. Meanwhile, why was I still in St-Tropez? Shouldn't I be back in Canada, celebrating Christmas in the snow? I said yes, I probably should be, but still had hopes of starting a novel. "A novel?" he said. "The only people who write novels are crazy people, like Plessi Toussaint. The only people who understand them are teachers, like me. The only people who read them are people escaping reality, and therefore wasting their time. Better you should seek a career in drama, or in pornographic films, where the real money lies."

Back at Le Gorille that evening, I found Plessi sitting at a table by himself, bleeding from nose and lip, both eyes blackened. Marius had given him an ice pack, which he held to the side of his face, and a straw, through which he gingerly sucked a martini. I suggested we take a taxi back to the clinic on rue Gassin, but he said it wouldn't be necessary. Though he had difficulty speaking, he let me know that had I gone with him to Crêperie Bretonne, he might not have been set upon by two belligerent motorcyclists, on their way from Toulon to Nice. They had stopped off at St-Tropez to visit an old friend, Yvette Chanteloup. Though they were there first, it was Plessi's contention that as a best-selling author and person of international importance, he had priority. Unfortunately, the young motorcyclists, hoodlums that they were—*vils bâtards*, he called them: misbegotten bastards—didn't see it that way. They hadn't read his books, had no idea who he was. To their faces, he called them *scélérats*, *canailles* (hoodlums, rabble), and when they protested, he made so bold as to raise his fists. Which, he now admitted, touching his split lip with a tentative finger, was not the best of ideas. It was, he said, like waving a red flag in front of a bull. To her discredit, Yvette Chanteloup had not lifted a finger to help him. She had in fact stood by while the two motorcycle thugs pummeled him about the head, knocked his glasses off, ejected him bodily from La Crêperie Bretonne. He doubted he'd ever go back. In the meantime, thanks to his publisher, who had forced him into exile in the first place, and thanks to Honoré Velmandois, who had thwarted his plan to visit Lise Escarène, and thanks to me, who had allowed him to be savaged by bullies, wasn't this one hell of a way to spend Christmas? "Marius," he said, raising his battered, swollen face, glaring balefully out of his discoloured eyes, "my one true friend, another martini with a straw, s'il vous plaît, and one for yourself."

"You should go to the police," I said.

"I would, mon gars, but Yvette threatens to inflict worse punishment if I do. The name of Crêperie Bretonne would be jeopardized. No good for her, no good for business."

Honoré Velmandois went to Marseille, a hundred kilometres away, by ambulance. He'd told us he was leaving on Saturday, but when Plessi and I went to say goodbye Friday evening, he was already gone. We had planned to ask him if he wanted one of us to accompany him, but his nurse assured us this would not have been possible, as no provision was made for a patient's friends to ride in the ambulance. In an emergency, a blood relative, perhaps, but a mere friend, no. It was a question of protocol, and of insurance. As to why he'd left a day early, with no word of farewell, she said that the St-Tropez doctors had no say in the matter. When the ambulance from St-Victor coronary centre in Marseille came for him Friday afternoon, Honoré had no choice but to go. In the meantime, did Plessi want his black eyes and contusions looked at? Emphatically, he said he didn't.

That Sunday, or possibly Monday, Plessi's literary friend, Lise Escarène, arrived unexpectedly in St-Tropez. She was on her way by bus from her villa at Agay to Nîmes, where she was to meet her husband, Rémy. Though they lived apart much of the year, she on the Riviera, he in Bordeaux, where he was curator of the Musée Archéologique, they always got together at Epiphany to celebrate their wedding anniversary. This year, they had chosen Nîmes for their rendezvous, because that's where Rémy was giving a series of lectures on Caesar Augustus and his famous three-tiered Roman aqueduct.

Rather than surprise Plessi at Filles du Soleil (she knew of his irregular hours and his vexation at being disturbed while working), Lise sent him a note by messenger from her posh hotel, Le Bombyx, on avenue Beau Rivage. The first I knew of this was when Plessi banged on my door one morning, came in uninvited, and sat on the edge of my bed. "Mon gars," he said, holding Lise's letter by one corner, as though it were something distasteful, "I have the problem. My friend Lise Escarène is in town, at Le Bombyx, and she invite me to dinner this evening."

"That's nice," I said, trying to wake up, wondering why, at this hour of the day, he was taking me into his confidence. "Since you couldn't go to her last week, she came to you."

"Non, mon ami, it is not nice. With this face, I cannot accept. She would laugh, everyone would laugh. It is not permitted to eat dinner at Le Bombyx with two black eyes and a broken nose."

"I didn't know your nose was broken."

"It may be. And lips that make me look like a Zulu. I would never recover my dignity. Questions would be asked. Someone from *Paris Match* would photograph us together. I cannot possibly go. I would be, what do you call it? the laughing stock. I have my reputation. Can you see the headline in *Le Monde*? 'Esteemed author, winner of le Prix Médici, but loser in a boxing match, dines out in St-Tropez with her highness, Lise Escarène.' Explanations would be required, shameful lies invented. Those two motorcycle assassins would take credit."

"I don't see why you're telling me all this."

"Because, mon gars, I must send you in my place. With my apologies. You must take a note to Lise from me, saying I'm indisposed, very sick. You will have a very nice dinner at Le Bombyx, a very nice chat about the writing of novels, which will be of more benefit to you than to me, since, to my knowledge, and looking around this pigsty of a room I believe it's true, in all the time you've been in St-Tropez, you've written not a word. Am I mistaken?"

Which is how I came to enjoy a four-course dinner and two bottles of Pommard '97 at Le Bombyx that night, in the company of Lise Escarène.

On my way to her hotel in a taxi, I read Plessi's note: "Ma chère Lise: Affligé d'une fièvre atroce, je dois garder mon lit. Terriblement désolé. En ma place, je t'envoie mon ami canadien, Guillaume, écrivain amateur mais ambitieux. Prends garde de lui, comme tu seule peux le faire. Je t'aime d'une tendresse extrême. A la prochaine: Toujours—Plessi." (My dear Lise: Afflicted with an atrocious fever, I must stay in bed. Terribly sorry. In my place, I send you my Canadian friend, William, an aspiring amateur writer. Look after him, as you alone can. I love you with extreme tenderness. Till next time: Always—Plessi.)

Le Bombyx is a large, quiet, luxury hotel in the suburbs, surrounded by olive and plane trees. It has a pink-marble façade, a pink-marble swimming pool, and a spacious garden full of flowering magnolias and pink-marble statues. At one time it was the château of a wealthy silkworm farmer. (I believe Bombyx is the Latin word for silkworm.) The foyer is hung with Raoul Dufy seascapes, interspersed with brass plaques and leopard skins. Persian carpets cover the pink-marble floors. Ceiling fans spin lethargically. The dining room, which is called Le Mouillage (I believe it refers to a ship at anchor), occupies the north side of the hotel. Its tall, tinted windows, framing ponds and fountains, face the Moorish Hills.

To me, Lise Escarène looked like a writer. I don't know why, exactly. Her eyes, behind oval spectacles, were constantly probing, searching. You could call her gaze intense. If she asked you a question, you felt compelled to answer it truthfully, because she seemed vitally interested. She was not what you would call glamorous, in that she obviously didn't spend a lot of time doing her hair or putting on makeup. Still, she had a pleasant, expressive face, where emotions were easily read. Her perfume was subtle, yet noticeable. She smiled often, said what was on her mind, laughed out loud. She had the curious habit of resting her chin on her hand and looking at you coquettishly, as though you were an old friend she hadn't seen in a while. Every so often, for no reason, she'd say, "Ayez pitié, mon cher." Have pity, my dear.

That night at Le Bombyx, she was wearing a colourful, loose-fitting blouse with the words "Jardin de Paris" printed across the front. As we sat at a table for two in a corner by the window and ordered our wine, she told me that while she was fairly comfortable speaking English (her husband Rémy was fluent, as were her two grown sons, Blaise and Rodrigue, who lived in Bordeaux), she preferred speaking French. Would that be a problem? I said it might be, depending on how fast she talked. Our silent, swarthy waiter, whose named was Christophe, and who was very young, either didn't know who Lise was, or pretended not to. We both ordered salade Niçoise, sea bream en papier and cassis sorbet. Without a word, Christophe went away and came back carrying two shrimp cocktails and a chilled bottle of Pouilly-Fuissé, compliments of an invisible maître d'.

The first thing Lise wanted to know, after asking me the titles of my books and telling me hers, was whether Plessi Toussaint was really sick. She seemed to expect the truth, and so I told her he wasn't, but had been in a fist fight with two motorcyclists.

"Over a woman?"

"Over Yvette Chanteloup, at Crêperie Bretonne."

"Is she beautiful?"

"Hardly."

"I'm not surprised. It's not the first time. Have pity, mon cher. Will he never learn?"

She then asked if he'd ever told me about the time two women attacked him with cucumbers in his Paris apartment, after a weekend spent celebrating his winning of the Prix Médici. I said no, he hadn't, but that I'd ask him about it. Lise thought he'd needed medical attention on that occasion. "Have pity, chéri. It must have been painful."

I told her that Plessi, Honoré and I had planned to visit her at Christmas, had even rented a car for the trip. She said it was a good thing we hadn't, because her villa was full of nieces and nephews on holiday from school and there wouldn't have been room. "Have pity, mon cher, but my house was bursting. I think I know this Honoré Velmandois you speak of, from articles in literary journals. I'm sorry he died."

"Oh, he didn't die, madame. He survived and was taken to St-Victor hospital in Marseille to recover. After that, he goes home to Paris, where I believe he may live with Plessi."

"You must call me Lise, chéri. Not madame. With Plessi Toussaint? How interesting. The novel writer and the novel teacher. A dangerous combination. They'll soon tire of each other, like a bad marriage. I'll pay them a visit next summer."

The fish in paper was succulent, the wine perfect. Christophe and his bus boy hovered, but not intrusively. While we ate, Lise told me things about Plessi I didn't know. She said he'd fathered a secret child, a boy, who was now in his thirties and lived in Rouen. His mother, Arianne, with whom Plessi had been briefly intimate, had told no one she was pregnant. The reason? She couldn't imagine ever marrying Plessi, who at that time was neither handsome nor wealthy. Consorting with him had been a miscalculation. The man she did wish to marry, whose name was Quiberon, was slow to propose. It was only after frantic seduction on Arianne's part that he finally did so. When the baby was born seven months later, Arianne named him Nicolas, after her father, from whom she hoped to inherit money, and convinced Quiberon that the child was his. After Quiberon's death twenty years later (he either fell or jumped off the Caudebec bridge in Rouen), Arianne encountered Plessi one day on Ile de la Cité in Paris, where they both happened to be visiting. She asked Plessi if he were married, and he said no, he was still a bachelor. Then she asked him if he had any children, and again he said no. "Eh bien," said Arianne, "that is not entirely true. You have at least one child—my son Nicolas."

Needless to say, Plessi was both saddened and thunderstruck. He was also somewhat skeptical, until Arianne showed him a photograph of Nicolas, in his sailor suit, and then he knew she was telling the truth.

As we started in on our cassis sorbet and chocolate cookies, Lise reached across the table and touched my hand. Not only touched it, but held it, caressed it. "If I were you, chéri, I wouldn't mention this to Plessi."

I refilled our wine glasses, hers with Pouilly-Fuissé, mine with Pommard. "Mention what?"

"That you know about Nicolas."

"And why not?"

"It's a subject he wishes to keep private, or so I've heard. Have pity, mon cher. Few people know about it. One must respect the privacy of one's friends. We are all entitled to our little secrets, especially in sexual and reproductive matters."

I remember wondering if I'd been missing signals. True, we were holding hands across the table. Hers was warm, soft, pliant. But it was when I looked into her eyes that I realized we'd gone beyond idle conversation. Unless I was grossly mistaken, there was invitation in her sultry glance, in the way she manipulated my fingers and reached across the table to detach a fleck of chocolate from my upper lip and place it on the tip of her tongue. I was dimly aware of Christophe lurking in the shadows, taking away empty bottles, talking softly to his bus boy. Distracted as I was, I hadn't seen him slip Lise the check for her signature. Only when she handed it back to him and let him pour the last of our wine did I realize the evening was nearly over. Actually, it wasn't over. It had barely begun.

"Tell me," Lise said, "are you yourself involved with this Yvette Chanteloup?"

"Not in the least. She's not my type."

"But she's Plessi's type?"

"Our tastes differ."

"Have pity, mon cher, but it's not uncommon for famous authors to share their women. Or so I've heard."

"But I'm not a famous author. As a matter of fact, I haven't written a word since I arrived in St-Tropez."

"I'm not surprised. I couldn't write here either. The only place I can write is in Paris, where life seethes and romance flourishes. Where people of all ages go to bed with each other and fuck like mink. Have pity, chéri, but would you like to see my junior suite? I believe we're finished here."

As though telepathic, Christophe emerged from the shadows, held Lise's chair for her, shook my hand, gave me a knowing wink.

I remember lying on Lise's queen-size bed (unusual for European hotels) and looking out the open window. The breeze coming in smelled of magnolias, even at this time of year. Or was it mulberries, favourite food of silkworms? The room was all in pink—pink curtains, pink bedspread, pink walls, pink bath tub, pink bidet. Or it may all have been due to pink light bulbs. Above the bed and on the opposite wall hung matching Raoul Dufy paintings, signed by the artist, showing the phallic-shaped St-Tropez lighthouse. In Dufy's day, the upper portion, where the flashing lamp is, was more rust than crimson. At least that's the way he painted it. His friend Picasso would probably have added a lugubrious eye.

When Lise came out of the bathroom, she still had her glasses on, but otherwise was stark naked. In the pink light, she looked fit and nicely tanned. I'd been lying there, thinking about her husband and two grown sons, and wondering whether Plessi Toussaint, if he were here, would be doing what I was about to do. Gently, Lise lay down on top of me, put her lips against mine, kissed me deeply. I believe I groaned. I could taste her toothpaste, but could no longer smell her perfume. Only her skin. She moved slowly, a millimetre at a time. What was it she'd said? In Paris, people of all ages go to bed with each other and fuck like mink. In St-Tropez too, evidently.

"Shall I tell you what famous women have stayed in this room, chéri?"

"How would you know that?"

"I've seen the guest book."

"Are they all French?"

"Some. Not all. You must lie very still."

"Are they famous because they stayed here, or were they famous first?"

"They were famous first. Annie Proulx, author. Alexa Lobran, actress. Ponty Glasse, biographer. Marie Lindroth, fashion designer. Jillian Hewitt, editor of Fodor's. Doris Lessing, author of *Walking in the Shade.* Helen Deachman, author of *Letters to Muriel.* Trish Pennebaker, graphic artist. Adam Gopnik, author of *Paris to the Moon.* I've forgotten the others."

"Adam Gopnik's not a woman. I've met him."

"Have pity, chéri. Of course he's not. I only mention him to see if you're paying attention. Now you may move."

✿

Hotel Sube, Café de Paris, St-Tropez

La Crêperie Bretonne, St-Tropez

Chapter Five

Next day, Lise continued her bus journey west to Nîmes, where her husband Rémy was waiting to celebrate their wedding anniversary. If she ever told me how long they'd been married, I've forgotten. Plessi didn't seem to know either. Not that it matters.

As for me, I took a taxi from the Bombyx to Filles du Soleil and was hauling myself upstairs to my room when I met Plessi coming down. He was on his way to breakfast at Le Gorille, after a good night's work on his Chirac book, and asked me to join him. Since I'd already had breakfast in Lise's suite (we'd sent down to room service for boiled eggs and melons), I declined. Besides not being hungry, I wanted to keep fresh in my mind the memory of waking up in Lise's capacious bed, with a delicious breeze ruffling the curtains and the chatter of magpies outside the window. We made love again before we ate, drank champagne and orange juice in the marble bath tub, took our coffee and cigarettes out on the balcony. The misty gardens were full of cats prowling among the statues. I wanted to retain these images.

Plessi said, "You look different, mon gars."

"I feel different. I may never be the same."

"I trust you spent an agreeable night?"

"I did, for which I thank you. I'm indebted."

"N'y a pas de quoi. Don't mention it. What are friends for? Did Lise ask about me?"

"Of course she asked about you. We spoke of nothing else."

"You told her I was sick?"

"I said you were at death's door."

"You didn't mention my black eyes or missing teeth?"

"I didn't know you had missing teeth."

"I could have. I'm afraid to look."

Because he seemed lonely, and because I realized I could use a rum grog to settle my nerves, but mostly because I wasn't sleepy, I accompanied him to breakfast at Le Gorille after all. In the harsh light of morning, he looked tired, haggard. The purple around his eyes was tinged with chartreuse. His split lip was less swollen, but the bruise on his cheekbone was shaded with green and yellow. It was hard not to laugh at him. Regulars coming in for their coffee and croissants, or their first pastis of the day, said hello to him, smiled sympathetically, asked him how he felt. Other than looking like a clown and keeping his chin lowered, he appeared to be on the mend. I asked him if he'd been back to see Yvette since the altercation, and he said he'd thought about it, but would wait a few more days. I told him that since it was all her fault, she should give him special treatment, at least a free appointment. Only then did he inform me that as a parting gesture, one of the motorcyclists had crunched his spectacles under his boot and kicked him in the groin. The memory of it made him wince, which hurt his face, which made him curse. "But the book is galloping like a runaway horse, mon gars. All I do is hang on and ride like the wind and try not to fall off. At such speed, I could hurt myself. If you were a serious writer, doing something useful with your life, instead of screwing married women, you would know what I meant. Did Lise give you pointers about the writing of novels?"

"She told me she could write about Paris only on the Riviera, and vice versa. She has to be at a distance."

Attacking his cheese omelet (his glasses might have been smashed and his groin kicked, but at least his appetite hadn't suffered), Plessi said, "I agree with that. I write much more objectively about Paris when I'm not there."

"Is it important to write objectively?"

"Of course it's important. Not only important, but vital. You must abstract yourself. Otherwise you become a writer of obituaries. How little you know, mon gars."

"Something else she said was that you never write about children."

He thought about this, took one of my Gauloises, signalled Marius for fresh grogs. "It's true, I don't."

"Are you afraid to?"

Wreathed in smoke, his discoloured face looked ghostly. His eyes, sunken in their dark sockets, were those of a defensive person. "I don't write about children because I lack experience with them. I've not had the pleasure or responsibility of rearing a child, so how could I portray one? The reader would see through me." He paused, drank half his grog in a single gulp, sucked greedily on his cigarette. "I've missed out on that aspect of life, mon ami. Through no fault of my own. At least none that I'd admit. But as to using children in books, they're not nearly evil enough for my purposes. Or if they are, it's instinctive rather than willful. A depraved child would not be convincing, and my characters are nothing if not depraved. As am I. Depravity is, how do you call it? my stock in trade."

Emboldened by my second rum grog (or was it my third?), I said, "Is it possible, Plessi, that you might have a child and not know it?"

He crushed out his cigarette, gave me a piercing, belligerent glower. "Lise Escarène has told you things she shouldn't have."

"Lise Escarène has told me nothing. I only meant that if you've been sowing wild oats half your lifetime, as you claim, then you might inadvertently ..."

"What is this, *wild oats*? Seeds?"

"Yes, seeds."

As so often happened at Le Gorille, even early in the morning, people at nearby tables were listening to us. Or at least to Plessi. Not because they were nosy, or inquisitive, but because they were interested. "Mon gars," he said, "the subject is close. Seeds, wild oats, who cares? That is in my past. I'm an old man now. Young men in boots and leather vests punch my eyes, break my glasses, give me fat lips. True, they will all appear in my next story, and not in a flattering manner. Once they attack me, I own them. They give up their rights to privacy. Without black eyes and hard knocks, I'd have nothing to write about. These confirm my belief in depravity. Everyone is depraved, but some hide it better than others. However, you must not ask me to discuss children, ever again. Despite what you say, I suspect you know things which I prefer to keep secret. They are none of your business. Nor of Lise Escarène's."

It grew quiet in Le Gorille after that, and once again I had the feeling of being in a theatre when the curtain comes down between acts. Marius stood off to one side, arms folded, looking thoughtful. Patrons began clamouring for their cappuccinos. Plessi and I had another rum grog, lit fresh cigarettes. The sun was up, mist was rising from the harbour. It showed promise of being a fine day on the Côte d'Azur. Sitting there, I experienced a pervasive contentment. It might have been the grogs, or the Gauloises, or the sun on the slowly swaying masts of a hundred stationary sail-boats. Or it might have been Plessi's presence. Poor, disfigured Plessi. Hurting, yet soldiering gamely on. Committed to his writing. Using depravity as a propellent. No wonder he was a best selling author and winner of the prestigious Prix Médici.

"You know, mon gars," he said, yawning, stretching his arms over his head, signalling Marius for the check, "some-day, we should go to Marseille and visit Honoré Velmandois. That would be a nice thing to do."

That afternoon, while Plessi slept, I wandered up and down the waterfront, from the lighthouse to the citadel and back again. Along the way, I stopped for drinks at La Jetée, La Marine and le Relais des Coches. I was surprised to discover a number of people doing the same thing. Whether they were residents enjoying the sun, or off-season travellers, who could say? Bars had their awnings raised, gulls were squabbling on the sea wall. Cormorants stood like sentries along the Customs pier, wings outstretched, drying their feathers. Artists sat at their easels, painting familiar scenes in unfamiliar light, capturing winter shadows and colours. Women with poodles on leashes strolled by. Cats I'd never noticed before were sunning themselves in nooks and crannies.

By evening, when it was time to meet Plessi for drinks and supper at Café de Paris (he was trying to avoid an obnoxious amateur writers' group who gathered once a month at Le Gorille, and who, he was afraid, would ridicule his black eyes), I felt carefree, but only mildly intoxicated, despite an entire day of drinking. Plessi said he'd slept poorly because of nightmares—dreams of being pursued down dark alleys and falling off bridges into murky rivers. With eyes wide open, he'd mistaken sunlight slanting through his shutters for flames, had jumped out of bed, thinking Filles du Soleil was on fire. He'd also dreamed that Honoré Velmandois was dead, and that Lise Escarène's husband, Rémy, a man he'd only met once, at a party, had gleefully brought him the news.

While he was telling me this, a blue Santa Azur tour bus, full of elderly tourists, stopped in front of Café de Paris and disgorged its passengers. There must have been twenty-five or thirty of them. Some used canes, some walked bent over, most moved slowly. As they made their way to a long table at the back of the restaurant, led by their tour guide, an officious woman in a burgundy blazer, Plessi said they looked like pilgrims in search of a shrine.

It turned out that's exactly what they were.

Their driver, a dapper, jowly man in a bright red sweater, sporting a neatly trimmed mustache, entered a few moments later and stood beside our table, looking for a place to sit. It was obvious he had no intention of joining his geriatric passengers. As the Café de Paris was crowded, and as Plessi evidently liked the look of the man, he tapped him on the elbow and invited him to occupy our extra chair. The driver appeared grateful, sat down, shook Plessi's hand. "Merci bien, monsieur. Vous êtes très gentil. Je m'appelle Umberto."

I think Plessi had forgotten about his bruises. When Umberto asked him if he'd been in a car accident, Plessi said no, a fist fight. Which made Umberto smile and look at him admiringly. He wouldn't have a drink, not even a glass of wine, but he ordered a large meal and several cups of coffee. He said that St-Tropez was not a scheduled stop on the tour,

McDonald's at the Louvre, a Burger King at Notre Dame. There's madness in the air. Basque terrorists blowing up metro stations. Muslim terrorists blowing up synagogues. Neo-Nazis blowing up mosques. Algerians killing Jews, Jews killing Arabs. Skinheads trying to shoot Jacques Chirac. Everyone I know who isn't afraid of volcanoes has gone to Guadeloupe. So I've come here."

"Without your wife?"

"My wife is dead."

"I'm sorry."

"Don't be. We were separated many years."

One of the old men beside us, in a fit of anger, accusing his opponent of cheating, suddenly picked up the backgammon board and hurled it out into the street. Then he stormed off in the opposite direction. His friend sat rigid, tears welling up in his eyes, and rubbed his hands over the empty table. His shame and sorrow and sudden loneliness were palpable. Baptiste came over and patted his shoulder, gave him a cigarette. Honoré ordered two more rum grogs, and one for the weeping old man.

"We were not meant for each other. She kept telling me that. Once, when she was sick in the hospital, I went to visit her, and she ordered me to leave. I never understood why. Then she went to Tahiti with a high-ranking official in the French Polynesian government, and I never saw her again. Every Christmas, she sent me a card bearing Gaugin's famous painting, Vision After the Sermon. One year, on my birthday, at great expense, she sent me a pagan idol with an enlarged penis. Soon after, I received an official letter saying she was dead and that our two adopted daughters had gone to live in Papeete with their step-father. So you needn't feel sorry. Could you manage another grog?"

That evening, when Plessi got out of bed and came down for his dinner at Le Gorille, Honoré Velmandois and I were quite inebriated. Or at least I was. I don't know how many rum grogs we'd had, but I could barely speak. I certainly couldn't but that the elderly passengers, after being on the bus all day, had clamoured for food and toilets. They were from a senior citizens' complex in Lyon, the Sanctuaire des Augustins, and were on a pilgrimage to Rome, where they had an audience with the Pope at St. Peter's next Wednesday morning. En route, they were visiting religious shrines, seeking spiritual uplift and cures for their aches and pains. They'd been to the grotto at Lourdes, which at that time of year was uncrowded, all but deserted. They'd crossed the Pyrenees into Spain and visited Santiago de Compostela. They'd been to Fatima, north of Lisbon, had seen pilgrims climbing stairs on their knees. Before leaving Portugal, they'd spent a morning at the Bom Jesus shrine in Braga, admiring the Fountain of Christ's Five Wounds. In Torino, Italy, they hoped to see the Shroud of Turin, and in Florence, the Basilica di Sante Croce.

From where we sat, we could watch the old people eating. They were talking, gesticulating, ignoring the tour guide, whose name, Umberto told us, was Madame Ste-Foy. She seemed to be arguing with her charges, many of whom had turned a deaf ear. The problem she was having, according to Umberto, was that from the very outset, beginning the day they'd left Lyon, the old people were disobedient. They had definite ideas about where they wished to go and what they wished to see. Unfortunately, they changed their minds every few hours. If they disapproved of Madame Ste-Foy's planned itinerary, they told her so. If they didn't like the hotels she selected, they demanded to be taken elsewhere. Likewise with restaurants and shops along the way. In the south of France, they'd insisted on bathing in the thermal waters of Bagnères du Luchon, even though the spa was fifty kilometres out of their way. There were three or four ringleaders (Umberto pointed them out to us at the long table— shaky, white haired men and women who looked docile, but who evidently were not), and it was to this committee that the others paid heed. Umberto said it had become a battle of wills. Every time they disagreed with Madame Ste-Foy, they voted unanimously against her. As tour director, she'd become powerless. When she tried to take charge, the old people banged their canes on the floor and threatened to throw her off the bus. Umberto said he felt sorry for her, but at the same time, admired the feistiness of the pilgrims. During Madame Ste-Foy's boring commentaries, they talked or slept or burst into song. The old men, especially those with weak bladders, demanded frequent rest stops, at which they would wander about, stretching, scratching, farting, while Madame Ste-Foy yelled at them to get back on the bus. Once, said Umberto, in northern Spain, after a day of bickering, Madame Ste-Foy had pleaded with him to take her side against the rabble. But he'd told her he didn't care where they went, or how long it took, because he got paid by the kilometre. France, Spain, Portugal, Italy—he had road maps for them all. Just pick your destination and he'd get you there. Madame Ste-Foy said she'd abandon the tour and go home, except that Santa Azur would probably dismiss her, because if she couldn't cope with a bus load of pensioners, what good was she to the company? They'd tell her to turn in her name tag.

Attacking his entrecôte and choucroute garnie (Santa Azur paid for his meals), Umberto said the crunch had come two days ago, when, after spending the night at Narbonne, Madame Ste-Foy had announced that from there they'd drive straight through to the Italian border. Which, once the news was relayed to the hard-of-hearing, had caused such a hue and cry and banging of canes, that Umberto had feared a mutiny. "Une révolte des invalides," he called it.

A spokesman for the group, an octogenarian named Saunier, one of the ringleaders, had told Madame Ste-Foy that unless they stopped at Monte Carlo and were given time to play the slot machines, they would stage a hunger strike.

"But Monte Carlo was never on the itinerary," Madame Ste-Foy retorted. "You can't simply add points of interest on a whim. Remember the other day, when you insisted we detour three hours off our track to see Cluny Abbey, and then when we arrived, no one would disembark because they thought they saw lepers in the cloister? There have never been lepers at Cluny Abbey. All that driving for nothing! Besides, this is a tour of religious shrines, not of gambling casinos. This is a pilgrimage to see the Pope. What will His Holiness say when you tell him you're late because you stopped off at Monte Carlo to play the slot machines?"

"The Pontiff would understand," Monsieur Saunier insisted. "One does not traverse the French Riviera without stopping at Monte Carlo. And who deserves good luck more than a pilgrim? God will smile on us."

"Then you should have mentioned this before we left Lyon."

"At our age, madame, one does not plan that far ahead. One day at a time. Why make plans and have to interrupt them for a funeral? If luck smiles on us, I will explain to the Holy Father that our contribution to his coffer, over and above the price of admission, is supplemented by our winnings."

"Sacrilege, Monsieur Saunier! You should be ashamed. His Holiness will demand contrition and a penance."

"His Holiness will demand nothing but the price of a ticket, madame. These days, with all the costly paedophile scandals in America, he has more on his mind than a few ancient pilgrims from the Augustin sanctuary in Lyon."

"This bus will not stop at Monte Carlo."

"If it doesn't, madame, we will exorcise you with our canes. How will that look on your résumé? How will you explain that to your superiors at Santa Azur?"

And so, having no other choice, Madame Ste-Foy instructed Umberto to stop at Monte Carlo, which he would have done anyway, rather than risk the ire (and the canes) of his strong-willed passengers.

"Look at them," he said to us, tucking into his profiterole with a fork and a spoon, signalling the waiter for yet another espresso. "You wouldn't believe the intrigues that go on. Do you see that thin old man beside Monsieur Saunier? He has designs on Madame Annecy, the lady across from him in the

big hat. Her husband, meanwhile, the man beside her in the
blue shirt and baseball cap, has stirrings for Madame
Pastèque, the lady at the end of the table in the flowered
dress. They sneak around at night, from room to room, feeling each other up. Can you believe it? I think they take too
many vitamins. It's not natural. At that age, they should be
relaxing. Their fornicating years should be over. Madame Ste-
Foy, as tour guide, pretends not to notice. But what could she
do? No one would believe her. Anyway, it's none of her business. Nor of mine. At Santiago de Compostela, I discovered
Monsieur Annecy behind a mausoleum with his hand up
Madame Pastèque's dress. In the beginning, when we left
Lyon, he had eyes for Mademoiselle Charentes, the spinster
lady with the silver handbag. But never having been married,
and not knowing any better, she repelled his advances. She
went to Madame Ste-Foy and reported him, and Madame
Ste-Foy told me to speak to him. Which I did, and he
stopped, which disappointed and frustrated Mademoiselle
Charentes, who regretted reporting him and wished she'd
kept her mouth shut. But it was too late. Monsieur Annecy
had found Madame Pastèque, who welcomed his hand up her
dress and was not in the least reticent. One wonders if these
people admit such things at confession. Probably not. En tout
cas, in a priest's eyes, they would be accomplishments rather
than sins, and praiseworthy.

So the new plan was to unload luggage, spend the night at
Hotel Sube, and leave next morning for Monte Carlo, which
they should reach in time for lunch. Hopefully, there would
be no requests for intermediate stops, say at Cannes, or
Antibes, or Cap-Ferrat. Plessi kept telling Umberto it was too
bad he couldn't have a rum grog or two, because he seemed
like the kind of man who would be likeable when tipsy. Plessi
himself had a red face by now, and slurred speech, and was
threatening to go over and give the old folks a sermon on
moral turpitude. But Umberto stuck to his guns, refused to
be tempted, saying that he knew from bitter experience he

couldn't stop at one drink, or two, or six, and that his contract with Santa Azur stipulated that he refrain totally from
alcohol while on the road. "And you're wrong, monsieur," he
said. "When drunk, I'm not a pleasant person. Unlike you
and your friend here, I become unreasonable. You would not
approve of me. Besides, I would lose my job. Madame Ste-
Foy would feel obliged to report me. Worse, I might try to
put my hand up her dress."

So when his passengers had finished their meal and
were straggling off to Hotel Sube, in search of their suitcas-
es and room keys, Umberto locked up his bus, bought an
Italian newspaper at the kiosk on the street.

The last thing Plessi said to him, before returning to
Filles du Soleil and his night's work, was, "Signore Umberto, do you know who I am?"

"Unless I'm mistaken," Umberto said, "you're the great
Plessi Toussaint, writer of defamatory novels."

Plessi smiled, happy to be recognized, shook Umberto's
hand. "Defamatory, but never malicious."

"I didn't say malicious, monsieur. I said defamatory."

"I may put you and your bus load of prehistoric pilgrims
into my next book. Would you mind?"

"It would depend, monsieur."

"On what?"

"On what you said about us."

"Then I may leave you out."

"That would be fine too, monsieur."

On our way home, Plessi and I stopped at Le Gorille for a
nightcap. It had been a long day, and I remember having
trouble keeping my eyes open. Plessi, by contrast, was energized, wide awake, eager to get on with his book. He said,
"One notices that you're drinking too much, mon gars. If you
keep this up, you'll develop the shakes."

"You're a fine one to talk. You drink more than I do."

"Yes, but I have more stamina, more experience. Also an
excuse. The alcohol lubricates my brain and allows me to

compose sentences which, sober, I'd never think of. You have no such need."

We were out of cigarettes, and so Marius brought us a packet of Gauloises with our final rum grog, which Plessi allowed me to pay for. I said, "If I stayed up all night and drank strong tea, could I compose nice sentences too?"

"I doubt it. You lack both compulsion and imagination. Looking at Umberto's passengers, would you have guessed they were depraved?"

"Never."

"You would not have cast them in bizarre stories?"

"I doubt it."

"Then give up the idea of becoming a writer. Go to bed at night and sleep, like normal people. Be a useful citizen of the world, like Umberto, like Madame Ste-Foy. Be a conformist, not an outcast like me, at whom people laugh and poke fun. You don't have enough, how do you say it? thick skin. You're afraid to be solitary, to stay up all night with your thoughts. Become a teacher, a useful public servant. It's much safer. Marry a normal Canadian girl. Raise normal Canadian children. Buy a normal Canadian car. Live in a normal Canadian house. Be ordinary. Resist the urge to analyse people. And don't drink so much."

"The only other Plessi I ever heard of was the Quebec premier, Maurice Duplessi. He was a tyrant too."

"A tyrant? I am many things, mon ami, but not a tyrant. If you must know, I was named after Armand du Plessi, otherwise known as Cardinal Richelieu, who insist on obedience to King Louis and defeat the Hapsburgs. Now that was a tyrant, mon gars. A man with ideas."

"Well, you have ideas."

"Having ideas does not make one a tyrant. A tyrant kills people. I believe you must be drunk."

"If I am, I have a right to be. I'm sure Cardinal Richelieu killed people. Maurice Duplessi might have too. And you kill people in your books."

At that, Plessi rose and went striding across the street to

Filles du Soleil. He was late getting to work. He had pages to write before morning. I sat at our table a while longer, alone, drinking a final rum grog, smoking a final Gauloise. I remember wondering whether Umberto would take me on his bus to Monte Carlo. To Florence. To Rome, where, for the price of a ticket, one could have an audience with His Holiness, the Pope.

I don't remember going home, climbing the stairs to my room on the second floor of Filles du Soleil, or getting into bed. Sometime during the night there was a freak thunderstorm, with flashes of green lightning over St-Tropez harbour. At one point, an excessively loud thunderclap and a brilliant bolt of lightning set off all the car alarms along the waterfront. The racket was unnerving and went on for a long time, keeping me awake. I imagined people running out in the rain, thinking someone was trying to steal their car. I listened for police sirens, but heard none. Next morning at breakfast, I asked Plessi if the car horns and thunder had disrupted his concentration.

"Not at all," he said. "I heard nothing, saw nothing. I was absorbed in my work."

"Did you have your shutters closed?"

"I usually leave them open at night. For the smells, which stir the memory, and for the air."

"And last night?"

"Last night I kept them closed, because of the wind."

"Then that explains it."

"Explains what, mon gars?"

"Why you didn't hear the thunder."

"Another explanation might be that there wasn't any."

When Marius brought us our eggs and cappuccino I asked him if he'd heard thunder and car horns during the night, and he said no, only sirens. "Look," he said, pointing at the dry pavement, the dry tables. "It was not raining."

Just then we saw the blue Santa Azur tour bus pulling away from Hotel Sube, on its way to Monte Carlo. It belched black smoke from its exhaust pipe. Plessi said he thought the pilgrims staring out its windows looked dazed, as though they had no idea where they were, or where they were going.

Honoré Velmandois

Le Gorille, St-Tropez

La Jetée, St-Tropez

Chapter Six

In the New Year, Plessi and I spent leisurely mornings at Le Gorille. We would start off indoors for breakfast, then take fresh grogs out to a table in the sun. It was pleasant there, talking, smoking, sipping our drinks. The town would be quiet till noon, with only church bells breaking the silence. People with hangovers would straggle in for coffee and cognac; and Marius, working alone, mixed raw eggs, vodka and Tabasco into a cure-all for the jitters.

Frequently, a group of children walked by, mostly boys, carrying fishing poles. They went out on the crumbling Customs wharf, displacing the cormorants, and threw baited lines in the water. From time to time they pulled in wriggling silver fish, not much bigger than sardines. What struck me was how serious they were, how intent. This was no child's game they were playing. This was no juvenile diversion. It may have been a contest of sorts, a demonstration of ability, but they applauded each other's success, gave credit where credit was due. If there was anything comical about their pastime, it was that they were all smoking cigarettes, trying to look mature as they baited their hooks and dropped their catches into plastic pails. Soon, they were surrounded by admiring girls, and resident gulls, squawking for handouts.

Plessi said it reminded him of his childhood in La Rochelle, an ancient seaport on the Atlantic coast, where two massive stone towers were built to guard the harbour when slave ships stopped on their way from Africa to the West Indies. He said his paternal ancestors had been involved in the slave trade, as shipping agents, and some of them had become wealthy. Some had been murdered too, and some had gone to Martinique as government officials. His grandfather, César, had been born there, and did not come to France (looking for a continental wife) until he was middle-aged. Plessi remembered his grandfather as a gruff, intolerant man, who smelled of tobacco and aniseed and disliked foreigners.

For two or three years, Plessi's father, an undistinguished solicitor, had taken his family to St-Malo, a walled city in Brittany, where they lived in a house once owned by the bloodthirsty pirate, Robert Surcouf. Monsieur Surcouf attacked passing Dutch and British ships, and allegedly brought nubile women ashore and kept them in his private dungeon. Plessi said he remembered playing in the dank dungeon with his siblings, tying them up to rings in the walls and making them beg for release. He said they used to take unsuspecting playmates downstairs and tie them up too, and show them where ruthless Captain Surcouf had tortured his prisoners and stored his treasure.

Plessi said he remembered being sad when the family moved back to La Rochelle, to a cold, austere house on rue du Palais, where his mother soon took sick and died and he and his sisters came under the guardianship of hysterical Aunt Lafaille. In time, Aunt Lafaille believed that the children were biologically hers, despite reminders from them that they weren't. As a troubled, short-tempered teenager, Plessi had run away to Ile de Ré, where he worked in vineyards and oyster fisheries. During this time, his father knew where he was, but was happy to be rid of him and left him alone. Then one day, hysterical Aunt Lafaille, fearing that Bérénice was possessed, beat her with a stick, blinded her in one eye, disfigured her face. So severe was the trauma that poor Bérénice was never quite right in the head. Eventually, she entered a Carmelite convent at Angoulème and Plessi lost contact with her, not seeing her until their father's funeral ten years later.

His other sister, Madeleine, a gentle girl with her father's looks and her mother's intelligence, had gone to Poitiers to become a nurse. Then to Troyes to become a teacher. And finally back home to become a journalist. As soon as Plessi finished his military service in Calais, he went to live with Madeleine in Châlons-sur-Marne, a hundred and fifty kilometres east of Paris. While there, at Madeleine's insistence, he'd obtained his certificat d'aptitude en anglais from the Institut Gallice, which would allow him entrance to a university. What he'd been doing in his spare time all those years, unbeknownst to anyone, was bury himself in libraries and read books. He worshipped writers like Victor Hugo, Emile Zola and Charles Dickens—men who told adventurous, believable stories. He said he began to feel a burning need to write such stories himself, and did, in classrooms, in cafés, in his bedroom at Madeleine's apartment, and later, in England.

When she was nearly thirty and afraid of becoming a spinster, or worse still, a nun, like Bérénice, Madeleine married a fellow journalist, a man named Palette, who worked for *Le Figaro* and had two mistresses, one in Louviers and one in Veules-les-Roses. He and Madeleine moved to Paris, to an apartment in the 7th arrondissement, with a view of the Eiffel Tower, but when Madeleine discovered the depth of her husband's dalliances, she hastened back to Châlons-sur-Marne. Pregnant but undaunted, she took up her old job and lost herself in work.

Meanwhile, Plessi had been living alone in a garret behind Cathédrale St-Etienne, working day and night on a rip-roaring novel of sex and violence, entitled *La Roukerie—The Rookery*. Its protagonist was a thinly disguised Etienne Mercier, crown prosecutor of Paris. who had been making newspaper headlines lately. Plessi said that when he showed the completed manuscript to Madeleine and asked for her professional opinion, she'd been shocked by the book's subject matter, but hugely impressed by its language and style. She made a few suggestions, which Plessi ignored, and showed the manuscript to a colleague at *Le Figaro*, the news editor, Jules Violette. After a single reading, Jules had sent the book to his friend Henri Barrage, a Paris agent, who, within a month, had sold it to Gallimard. Henri Barrage informed Jules Violette, who informed Madeleine, who informed Plessi, and the rest, as they say, is history.

The day *La Roukerie* was published, Madeleine gave birth to a baby girl, Balanéa. It was, Plessi said, as though he and his niece had found their voices at the same moment. With access to *Le Figaro's* archive of microfilm, he researched sensational stories about dignitaries and dashed off two more books in his Châlons-sur-Marne garret, *Vilebrequin* and *Nébulaire*, neither of which, unfortunately, was as well received as *La Roukerie*. In fact, critics called them juvenile and disappointing, the product of a callow author who should travel and gain experience in life before attempting any more books. Otherwise, Plessi Toussaint might forever be known as a one-book author, *un feu de paille*, a flash in the pan.

The morning he told me this, as empty glasses accumulated in front of us, it became apparent, to me at least, that Plessi was in no hurry to go home. The more grogs he drank, and the more I probed, the deeper he sank into reverie. He seemed to be enjoying himself, even if the memories he dredged up were not entirely benign. As the youthful fishermen out on the Customs wharf became more animated and began playing tag, I told Plessi I thought his childhood had been useful and interesting. Compared to mine, which was boring beyond belief. While I carried no permanent scars, neither did I have his wealth of experience to draw on.

He thought about this, expropriated my entire pack of Gauloises. "It's because of the crazy, evil people of my childhood, mon gars, that I am, how do you say… all screwed up." He took off his glasses, polished them with a paper napkin, as though hoping to see more clearly. "My Aunt Lafaille was a mad woman who belonged in an asylum."

"The aunt who beat your sister?"

"The very one. To drive out the devil. She beat Bérénice on the legs to make her dance, on the head to hurt her. 'Sortez, maudit morveux!' Come out, damned evil. Release this child from your clutches. Oh, see the devil's contortion. That's proof he's in there. Sortez, Satan! Come out through the eye, the way you went in."

He said that when he himself reached puberty, at the age of the energetic young fishermen on the Customs wharf, Aunt Lafaille had taken it upon herself to warn him of the perils of masturbation. It was a practice she knew nothing about, but suspected he was engaging in. Not only because of his stained bedsheets, but because she watched him through the keyhole of the bathroom door. She would also burst into his bedroom, brandishing a flashlight, *une lampe de poche*, shouting that if she ever caught him touching himself she'd cut off his penis and fingers with a carving knife. Lest he minimize the horrors of autoerotism, she dragged him by the ear into the street and showed him the town hunchback, Monsieur Bellecroix, a deformed and crippled old man who walked doubled over, chin level with his knees, unable to see where he was going, eyeballs straining upward. "Look, Plessi," she'd said. "That fate awaits you if you indulge in this unholy, forbidden action. You will become *un bossu*, a hunchback, like this man, who, as a boy your age, fell victim to just such habits. It is God's curse on him, and he will punish you similarly. There is no escaping it. What you're doing will make you insane and curve your spine. You will develop crippling arthritis, tuberculosis, leprosy. Your teeth will turn black and fall out. They will put you in chains and lock you away. You will never see your beloved aunt again, who prays for your soul. Or your beloved father, who would be ashamed of you. Or your sisters, whom God will punish in other ways for their disobedience."

While his aunt's dire warnings caused Plessi to abstain for a week, they did nothing to diminish his nocturnal emissions, over which he had no control and which left incriminating evidence. Nor, when he resumed the voluntary practice, on a trial basis, vowing to desist at the first sign of deformity, did they prevent him from making up for lost time. He said that during those years, even though burdened with guilt, he'd ejaculated enough semen to repopulate the entire planet, several times over. Despite which, his spine hadn't bent, he hadn't gone crazy, nor had he grown hair on the palm of his hand.

Still, Aunt Lafaille's remonstrations had affected him, had affected his sex life and given him nightmares. Not until he went to Calais to serve his two years in the army, and was introduced by the regimental chaplain to far more aberrant pastimes than self-arousal, did his hangups begin to fade.

I remember how he sat quietly for several minutes, thinking, remembering, shaking his head. He took a gulp of grog, lit a fresh cigarette. With his eyes closed, he said, "I should probably not tell you this, mon gars, but if I'm screwed up sexually, so are my sisters, and mainly because of our father and Aunt Lafaille."

He stopped, watched the boys fishing, said hello to an old woman walking her spaniel. I thought he might have decided to call it a morning, but then he said that his father, when drunk, as he often was, would force himself on Madeleine, his own daughter, in the bedroom she shared with Bérénice, and if Bérénice woke up, he forced her to watch what he was doing to Madeleine. It didn't matter that both girls wept and shouted at him. Nor that they threatened to tell their aunt what a monster he was. Indeed, it was when Bérénice had gone to Aunt Lafaille with her complaints that she'd been beaten and had her eye put out. Aunt Lafaille had called her a witch, deserving of death by stoning. No wonder she'd entered a convent. No wonder Madeleine had waited so long to marry, and even then had chosen an adulterer. The whole family was screwed up sexually. He said that had he been born female, he'd have turned out like Yvette Chanteloup—good hearted, yet eager to subjugate men, tie them to rings in the dungeon, while making them pay for their pleasure.

After Marius had refilled our grogs and brought us saucers of prawns, Plessi admitted to a prolonged affair with the regimental chaplain in Calais, Father Dampierre. He was older than Plessi, and had slit his wrists with a razor blade after Plessi told him he could not continue the physical relationship, for fear of being discovered and humiliated. And also because he no longer loved the priest. In fact, there was a pretty woman in Calais, a married woman he'd met at the cinéma, for whom he felt an overpowering physical and emotional attachment. The last he saw of Father Dampierre, the military police were taking him away to have his wrists bandaged. He was sobbing and calling out to Plessi, pleading with him, but Plessi had turned his back.

He'd had his own brush with the law when he returned to Châlon-sur-Marne and had lured a young girl up to his garret and attacked her when she pretended not to know what he wanted. He'd lost his composure, he said, ripped her clothes off, hit her when she began shrieking, couldn't stop himself. Finally, after ravishing her as best he could, he'd let her go, and an hour later two policemen, in boots and leather jackets, had pounded up his stairs and arrested him. He'd spent three months in confinement, had been forced to attend corrective lectures, and had been released only on condition that he leave Châlons-sur-Marne. Not only did he leave Châlons-sur-Marne, he left France, and taught conversational French at a girls' school in Wembley. From there, he'd had to hurry away, one step ahead of the *Brigade des moeurs*— the vice squad. While in England, at Madeleine's suggestion, he'd tried newspaper reporting, and was reasonably good at it, but, as he told Ms Langtry, his lesbian boss at the *Evening Standard*, what he really wanted to do was write books. It was his calling. To that end he spent his spare time jotting down, for future use, profiles of deviant, disturbed people.

"So you see, mon gars," he said, "I am, how do you say? a fucking nut case when it comes to *ardeur sexuelle*. I'm lucky to be alive. Yet these encounters are useful for my books, because what quirks I have, others have too. I request Madeleine to search for crackpots on *Le Figaro's* computer, and there I have my characters. Names, dates, details. Imagination on my part is not required."

I wondered how much of what he'd told me was imaginary. Surely some of it. The longer we sat there in the sun that morning, the more relaxed we both became. There were whitecaps beyond the breakwater and soaring gulls. The adolescent fishermen had departed, leaving the Customs wharf to the cormorants. A large orange cat came wandering by, jumped briefly into Plessi's lap for a scratch and a prawn or two, then jumped down and ran after a finch in the hedgerow. Plessi seemed unconcerned about sleep, even though he'd been awake for eighteen hours. I remember he said, "So this is how you spend your day, mon gars. Sitting around talking of old times. Accomplishing nothing. Keeping Marius company and getting drunk. It's a life one could get used to, but not a good life. In Paris, in winter, you can't do this, sit exposed to the sun, reminiscing with friends. For one thing, the sun is hidden in perpetual overcast. For another, people are busy working. They're going somewhere by car or by métro, taking lunch at Brasserie Lipp or Les Deux Magots. They're having meetings with their agents, or looking up facts at the Bibliothèque Nationale. Always something important to do. And after all that, one either sleeps or rides the bus across town from Neuilly to Montparnasse."

Sipping a fresh grog, tripping over my words, I asked him if he'd ever tried a genre other than his so-called novels. He said he'd once tried his hand at science fiction, but without success. One of his stories, entitled *Nervation*, had been about an invasion of earth by aliens in an amorphous spacecraft. Its passengers had been spineless, blob-like creatures, fleshy extensions of the mother ship. They had as many arms as we have fingers, as many legs as we have toes. Their faces had been where our genitals are located, their genitals where our heads are. Their voices were halfway between cats purring and frogs croaking. They'd come to earth, it transpired, looking for food and diversion. They'd been away from home eons in our time, moments in theirs, had visited six hundred galaxies and sent back reports on every one. "What a pain in the ass," their spongy leader had said, or at least intimated.

They weren't interested in precious metals, water, or nuclear reactors. What they found interesting were whales and obese humans, as nourishment. Of the two species, neither of which was entirely to their liking, they preferred humans. Just as some people prefer Brie to Camembert. It's a matter of taste. Consensus was that if they took a few humans home with them (just as Charles Darwin had taken Jemmy Button and his wife home to England from Tierra del Fuego), they might, through genetic engineering, breed a better tasting version. They took a few Frenchmen on board to see what elements they were composed of, and therefore what kind of atmosphere they'd need on the voyage to the other side of the universe. Among the scientists an argument broke out as to whether Frenchmen were the best tasting. Again, like Brie versus Camembert. Or pork versus beef. Or fish versus chicken. Finally it was decided they'd test a few Germans, a few Italians, a few Spaniards, a few Turks, a few Scandinavians. There was debate as to whether men or women were more palatable. And whether broiling was preferable to roasting. And whether the skin was better left on, like a new potato, or removed, like an onion. The final outcome of all this palaver was a consensus among the testers that plump Italian women tasted best, closely followed by Peruvian men. Midway down the scale were Scottish children, and at the very bottom, Belgians of either sex. Colour of skin didn't matter. They all crisped nicely on the gamma ray grill. Of course there were allergies to contend with (Swedes gave some people gas, others got hives from Lithuanians), but this was not a major problem. The main thing was concocting the right sauce and deciding what veggies to serve with a haunch of Greek.

Plessi said he was not surprised when Gallimard and several other publishers turned down *Nervation*. Not that it was badly written, they said, or too far-fetched, but they felt Plessi Toussaint's career as a serious social commentator might be jeopardized by the release of such a book. Better to stick to what he was known for—exposing celebrities as tainted hypocrites. This was his forte. It's what readers expected from him, what they paid good money to read. Leave science fiction to those whose names were associated with make-believe: Brugmann, Heseltine, Azeglio. You didn't see Paul Theroux writing science fiction. Or Peter Mayle. Or Mordecai Richler. Plessi Toussaint should stick to what defined him. A little satire would be acceptable. Lots of sex, a bit of humour, a few accusations, so long as they were well founded. A little personal reaction to world calamity. But science fiction? Not really. Not unless he used a pen name.

It was mid-afternoon before we left Le Gorille. Marius and the other waiters were busy serving lunch and drinks, both indoors and out. Older men were now fishing on the Customs wharf. Compared to the children, they were silent, brooding. They smoked, coughed, drank from thermos jugs. Every so often one of them would hawk and spit into the harbour. They seemed to catch fewer fish than the boys, or perhaps they just made less fuss.

It had been a fascinating, illuminating, if not totally believable morning, listening to Plessi, drinking rum, smoking Gauloises. The only trouble was, I could scarcely walk. Noting my condition, Plessi let me lean on him, helped me across the street to Filles du Soleil. "Mon gars," he said, a little thickly I thought, "unless you learn to drink in moderation, especially this early in the day, I don't know what's going to become of you."

Then we both stumbled, but didn't fall. Cars stopped and waited for us, as well they should have. Once safely across, we bowed to them and Plessi waved his hat. Some drivers tooted their horns. Some rolled down their windows and shouted at us, as they do in Paris, Toronto, or New York. Others raced their engines and sped off down the street.

I vaguely remember crawling up the stairs and Plessi saying, "Do you think, mon gars, we should wake Monsieur Nemours?"

"Whatever for?"

"To ask him if he need to take the piss."

"I think that would be a bad idea. Since it's mid-afternoon, he's probably already pissed."

"To hell with him then?"

"Yes, to hell with him. I'm afraid you won't get much writing done today."

"Mon gars, I won't get any writing done today. Have you forgotten? I sleep all day and work all night. It's you who won't get much writing done today."

"I'm sorry to hear that."

"So am I, but I can only do so much on your behalf. I will say one thing for you, you're a good listener. Someday you must tell me about your own childhood, and who you blame for all your faults."

"Faults, Monsieur Toussaint? I have no faults."

Which made him laugh, as he pointed me at my door and continued on up the stairs to his own room. "Then you had no childhood, mon gars. Anyone who had a childhood has faults. If you were a serious writer, you would know that."

Lise Escarème

St-Tropez Marina

Chapter Seven

I thought Plessi might have been an old suitor of Lise Escarène, from before she was married. But he wasn't. He said they'd been thrown together for the first time in 1990, at a writers' conference in Paris.

We were having breakfast at Le Gorille one February morning, and he said the day reminded him of June in Paris, when the spring rains are finished and chestnut trees on boulevard St-Germain are in flower. In another month, you'd notice the heat. And the smells. And barge traffic on the Seine. And swarms of tourists, as buses crowded the narrow streets. Germans and Japanese and Americans would invade like locusts, posing for group photos at the Eiffel Tower, at the Arc de Triomphe, at the Louvre. Tours led by multilingual guides would infiltrate Notre Dame and the Palais de Chaillot. Luxembourg Gardens and Les Invalides, oases of calm during the winter, would be overrun. Place Pigalle and all of Montmartre would reverberate with street musicians. Artists would be stationed on quai d'Orsay and at place du Trocadéro. Restaurants all over town, but especially on the Left Bank, would be packed. Bug-eyed drunks would stagger out of all-night strip clubs in Montparnasse. You'd hear more English than French spoken on quai de la Tournelle as you meandered among the bouquinistes and flower-sellers. In July and August, native Parisians would head north, south and west, toward salt water, anywhere to escape the heat and the tourists. They would not return until September, by which time it would be noticeably cooler and the days shorter. Or so Plessi said. On that quiescent morning at Le Gorille, Paris seemed a continent and ten time zones away.

He said it was in June that the big Paris publishing houses (Gallimard, Hachette, Vendôme, Belfond, Tallandier, Edimedia, Solange Shwarz) got together and hosted a two-day writers' conference. You couldn't just show up and expect to be admitted. Like the Cannes Film Festival, you had to be invited. There were talks, readings, workshops. In 1990, the event was held at two hotels—the Intercontinental on rue Castiglione and the Meurice, right around the corner, on rue de Rivoli.

At that time, Plessi was living in a 5th-floor studio on boulevard de Sebastopol, a mere twenty-minute walk from the Meurice. Other delegates to the conference were housed at the Ritz, the Montpensier and the Gaillon-Opéra. Lise Escarène was at the Gaillon-Opéra, in a room with another female author, Ambroisie Pacaud, better known to the reading public as Anne Cagouille. Her claim to literary fame was *La Fourmi Blanche (The White Ant)*—a shocking, unauthorized biography of Edith Piaf, which came out in 1988 and caused a stir. Lise Escarène had also published an unauthorized biography that year, *Le Muscardin (The Dormouse)*, detailing the indiscriminate couplings of François Philidor, 18-century chess master, composer of opéras, and enormously endowed stud. Her book on Philidor, though praised by critics, didn't do nearly as well as Anne Cagouille's on Edith Piaf, because she was less well known.

The first afternoon of the conference, both ladies attended Plessi Toussaint's seminar on "Un nouveau vocabulaire pour décrire l'acte sexuel entre deux adultes en commun accord." (A new vocabulary for describing sexual congress between two consenting adults.)

Thinking back to this workshop, sipping a rum grog after breakfast at Le Gorille and puffing his usual Gauloise, Plessi said he remembered two main problems. First, after partying all night with Eugène Bordet, the renowned Belgian novelist, he'd been terribly hung over, or possibly still drunk. And second, he kept getting off topic. As Lise pointed out to him at the end of the day, his new vocabulary went far beyond two participants, and made provision for as many as eight. Of any age. Nor did there have to be consent. Nor was there anything new about the words and phrases he advocated.

Plessi told me he hadn't meant to offend anyone, least of all his fellow authors. He thought they'd take his spiel lightly, ironically, in the spirit in which it was intended. But some didn't. As with his books, there were repercussions. A few prudish people walked out. Others tittered. No one appeared to be on his exact wavelength. No one, that is, except for two attractive ladies in the front row, wearing short summer skirts and low-cut blouses. At intermission, they introduced themselves: Lise Escarène and Ambroisie Pacaud. They said they found his new vocabulary fascinating. Which was not surprising, since they found his books fascinating too. How did he come up with all these exciting ideas, all this erotic terminology? Surely not from real life?

Yes, from real life. From his family. From a perverted parish priest in Calais, Father Dampierre. From a Wembley girls' school. From *la caserne*—army barracks. From the microfilm library of *Le Figaro*, where everything was in black and white. Wasn't that the secret of good writing? Describing real people, in real situations, suffering real consequences? And wasn't lust a universal theme? Of course it was. Not to be eclipsed by hate, betrayal, guilt and jealousy, mind you, but right up there near the top.

After the intermission, Plessi brought in Benoît Dômarais and his mute girlfriend, Jo Bofinger, acclaimed Parisian puppeteers. They stood behind a curtain and staged a funny, pornographic show entitled *Chatouille-Sans-Rire* (literally: *Tickle Without Laughing*, but of deeper meaning to Frenchmen). Several contortionist puppets translated Plessi's lecture into obscene ballet. Benoît Dômarais did the voices and sound effects. You could see why he had the reputation of being the best pornographic puppeteer in all of Paris, and there were many. The audience responded with gasps and laughter. Only a few unappreciative prigs departed. When it was over, and all the marionettes lay exhausted on stage, there was rousing applause. Remembering the event, Plessi chuckled to himself, clapped his hands gleefully, signalled Marius for fresh grogs. "Mon ami," he said, "it was a masterpiece.

They should hold such puppet shows here in St-Tropez. Mine in Paris that year was a great success, the highlight of the conference. It got my point across. You see, the marionettes were anatomically correct and painted to look like real people—the président and his wife, the minister of culture and his mistress, the foreign minister and his boyfriend, the ambassador to Spain—all tangled together in a fine, comic orgy. You should have seen it. It still brings me joy. Benoît the puppeteer took ten bows. Had his actors been live, it couldn't have been more realistic. And the music! And the singing! Mon gars, it should have been on television. The Marquis de Sade would have been proud, Henri Miller ecstatic."

After the puppet show, Plessi and his friend Eugène Bordet had accompanied Lise Escarène and Ambroisie Pacaud to the Gaillon-Opéra for drinks. They had dinner in the courtyard, hovered over by waiters dressed like penguins, then went for a stroll in the Tuileries Gardens, where lovers lounged on the grass or boated on a pond lit by floodlamps. After that they went back to the hotel, had champagne sent up to the room, and, in Plessi's words, reenacted as much of the puppet show, "Chatouille-Sans-Rire," as they could remember. At midnight, Eugène Bordet had lost consciousness with a smile on his face and they continued without him.

Next day, if you can believe Plessi, and I do, he and the two ladies drove to Versailles in Ambroisie Pacaud's Porsche. They had lunch, then drove south to Fontainebleau, where they registered at the Hôtel de Londres as a brother and two sisters. Next day, they drove to Soissons for a river cruise, and the day after that back to Paris, where they found Eugène Bordet still at the Gaillon-Opéra, in bed with a chambermaid. They also found Plessi Toussaint's name in all the papers, as winner of an award for the most morally corrupt author of the decade. His official title, on a trophy presented to him a week later by Guy Beauharnais, secretary of La Société des Ecrivains Gaulois, was, "Homme de Peu de Moralité"—Man of Loose Morals.

Before we left Le Gorille that morning to go our respective ways, Plessi and I were visited by two priests. They approached our table unhurriedly, stopping to talk to Marius and others, but heading in our direction.

I recognized one of them. I believe his name is Father Le Coz. He's a man of about sixty, plump, ruddy-faced, benevolent-looking. I'd seen him while wandering the streets, and coming out of his church, Notre-Dame de L'Esterel, on rue des Blancs Manteaux. In his robes and ankle boots, he struck me as a kindly, concerned man, always smiling at you, saying hello, willing to stop and talk if that's what you wanted. I never did, but often thought it would be rewarding. He was accompanied that morning by a large, corpulent priest, whose cassock didn't quite hide his belly. While you would have pegged Father Le Coz as friendly, his colleague wore a severe, unsmiling expression, as though he were on a tour of inspection and didn't like what he saw. At first glance, he struck me as someone who enjoys criticizing, threatening, making recommendations. Plessi said later he thought this might have been the Bishop of Monaco, making his rounds of the diocese. He said he'd arrived the day before in a chauffeur-driven limousine.

As the two priests made their way toward us, it was intriguing to see how some people turned away from them, while others stood up and shook hands. Father Le Coz appeared to be making introductions, patting his parishioners on the head. I'm sure he would have liked to sit down and enjoy an iced cassis. However, the closer he got to our table, the more agitated Plessi became. I'd never seen him like that. He kept his eyes riveted on Father Le Coz, like a cobra watching a mongoose. He finished his drink, stubbed out his cigarette, as though preparing to flee. I had the distinct impression that the bishop, if that's who he was, recognized Plessi, or wanted to meet him. I also had the impression, from Plessi's body language, that he intended to avoid this. I could picture Father Le Coz being placed in an awkward position.

Suddenly Plessi stood up, motioned me to follow, walked away in the direction of Le Relais des Coches. He might have headed for Filles du Soleil, except that his way was blocked by the approaching priests. I had time to notice the surprised look on Father Le Coz's face. I think his feelings were hurt. I'm sure he felt snubbed, embarrassed. The bishop had obviously asked for an introduction to this prominent author, though for what reason, who could say? I remember feeling sorry for Father Le Coz. He was a nice man and didn't deserve to be treated rudely.

When I caught up to Plessi at Le Relais des Coches, he'd already found a table and ordered our grogs. "Did you see that, mon gars?"

"See what?"

"That Bishop of Monaco bearing down on me."

"I saw Father Le Coz and another priest greeting parishioners. Why do you think they were bearing down on you?"

"They were. Trust me. They were about to tell me my soul was in jeopardy because of the things I've written in my books about psychotic priests. All true, by the way."

"If you say so."

"It's something I don't need. Not right now. I have my mind full. There's no room for penitence."

I wasn't sure what to say. Here was a chink in Plessi Toussaint's armour I hadn't expected. He'd already finished his first grog and ordered a second before I'd taken my first sip or smoked my first cigarette.

"The witch doctor and his *marguillier adjoint.*"

"His what?"

"His churchwarden. His, how do you call it… sidekick."

"That seems a bit judgmental."

"One thing I don't need is my soul saved. They'd like to censor me. For a price, they would sell me absolution."

"Is that what you're afraid of?"

"I'm afraid of nothing, mon ami. Not even of purgatory. I'm too old to be afraid. I have books to write. I won't be silenced by anyone. Not by a pot-bellied priest in a soutane who steals minds from people and sells forgiveness."

"I don't follow. How does a priest steal minds?"

"Mon gars, your stupidity amaze me. Everything he says is hoax and superstition. He's *un fumiste*, an impostor. A bigger liar even than me. He will baptize you, marry you, sprinkle water on your coffin, in exchange for money and your soul. He need your soul to feed his ego, your money to let him live richly in the palais épiscopal, secure from brouhaha and agitation. He have a good life, chasing nuns and altar boys, getting drunk on ecclesiastical wine, fat on ecclesiastical honey, while his parishioners go into debt and starve."

I suppose I could have provoked him by accusing him of exaggeration, or by saying I saw nothing wrong with all that, but given his present state of mind, I thought it best to keep quiet. I said, "Maybe Father Le Coz just wanted to say hello and introduce you to the bishop."

Plessi was so intent on looking over my shoulder to make sure we weren't being followed, that I doubt he heard me. As calm descended, we sat back to enjoy the morning and our drinks. I was dimly aware of people walking by and greeting Plessi by name, and of him not responding. Finally, he said, "My sister Bérénice lives in a convent, you know."

"Yes, you've told me."

"I can't imagine a loneliness like hers. It's a good thing she's in a convent, with other lonely people."

Feeling mildly argumentative, I said, "Maybe they're not lonely."

"Of course they're lonely. How could they not be lonely? They have no one to talk to."

"How about you? Are you lonely?"

"Sometimes. Not always. Not when I have work to do. In my old age, when I no longer write books, I may be lonely. When I'm on my deathbed, I may be lonely. I won't be surrounded by a loving wife and children, as one is supposed to be, because I have no loving wife and children. I'll have only my cold books to surround me. Books to which I've devoted my life. Then I may be lonely."

"In your room at night, all by yourself, who do you talk to?"

"I talk to my word processor. Like my sister talks to God. Except that my word processor is real. I can see it."

"Is your other sister lonely?"

"Madeleine? No, she has her daughter. And colleagues. It's ironic, don't you think, that Bérénice is being punished for what she saw, while Madeleine, who suffered the abuse, has a daughter and a purpose in life."

I found this intriguing. We both started in on fresh grogs, although Plessi was two or three ahead of me. "Are you saying that Bérénice has no purpose in her life?"

"Well, what purpose could she have? She lives in a nunnery and has only one eye. She's never worn a patch, you know. Aunt Lafaille wanted her to. She said a priest told her the devil came out of that eye, and Bérénice should wear a patch, so he couldn't get back in. Poor Bérénice. So timid, so withdrawn. And not her fault. She was blameless, and now she's in a nunnery, a grown woman with the mind of a child. She didn't progress from the day Aunt Lafaille blinded her. When I leave here, I'll go and visit her. Even if she no longer knows me. Even if it break my heart."

That tranquil morning was the one and only time I ever saw Plessi Toussaint shed tears. He shed them only briefly, and not very many, before getting a grip on himself. He wasn't crying in his beer, he was crying in his rum grog. And all because his sister Bérénice lived in a convent. Or because Father Le Coz had wanted to introduce him to the Bishop of Monaco.

I walked him back to Filles du Soleil, and while he went up to bed I detoured into the book shop on the ground floor. After a moment's browsing, I asked the clerk, Madame Jean-Goujon, to sell me Plessi Toussaint's best book. That would be difficult, she said, because Monsieur Toussaint's books were all good. Well, which would she recommend? She would recommend no fewer than two. For example, let's say, *Jocrisse* and *Condamné*. But *La Roukerie* and *Magnéto* were good too. She had them all. But of course only in French. She didn't sell translations. Other book stores might, but they were very expensive and of mediocre quality. You didn't get what you paid for. And why, since I lived upstairs, a floor below the author himself, had I waited so long to purchase his books? And did I know that he'd been approached a year ago in Paris to put his books on tape? It was the newest fad. And Plessi had agreed, but on the appointed day he'd arrived at the recording studio too drunk to stand up, never mind talk into a microphone. And so the contract had been cancelled. A new, sober reader was being sought, but to date, none had been found. At least none suitable, with a rich voice and strong Parisian accent. If I came back in the fall, I might find something.

In the end, I bought paperback editions of *Jocrisse* and *Condamné*. It was such a beautiful day that I wandered out on the Customs pier, found a sunny spot protected from the wind, and sat down to read. As with my earlier attempt at *Crédillon*, however, I found the task difficult. I would have needed a dictionary. The language was too idiomatic for me, too full of slang and blasphemy. And so I soon gave up. Besides, reading the books of an author who lived in my building and with whom I ate breakfast and drank rum grogs, seemed pointless. Why not just talk to him? I found myself daydreaming, thinking of poor one-eyed Bérénice in her nunnery. What must her life be like? Was she bitter?

While I sat there, soaking up sun, watching the activity ashore and in the harbour, I noticed a crippled youth of sixteen or so limping slowly along the pier. He was wearing a dark coat and carried a fishing rod. He went by me without speaking, dragging one bad foot, and although I said hello to him, he didn't answer. I wondered if he were deaf. At the end of the pier he cast his line and reeled it in slowly. I was struck by what a lonely figure he made, out there all by himself. Like Bérénice, with no one to talk to or share the experience. It was quite sad. Unlike the gang of boys we'd seen fishing there, this young man seemed to derive no pleasure from his pastime. I wondered why he bothered. Why stumble all that distance, dragging one foot, just to throw a line in the water? It made no sense.

For reasons which I can't begin to explain, I walked over to him and handed him Plessi's books. "Have you read these?" I asked.

He looked at the books, shook his head.

"Have you heard of the author, Plessi Toussaint?"

Again he shook his head.

"Would you like these books? As a gift? If you want them, they're yours. I'm sure they're very good, but I can't understand them."

He looked at me, and at the books, and for a moment I had the horrible notion that he was retarded. But he wasn't. "Merci beaucoup, monsieur," he said, very softly. "Vous êtes bien généreux."

To my dismay, he put the books in his pocket, reeled in his line, and went limping back along the pier toward the old Customs house. When he reached it, he looked back, nodded several times, waved the fishing pole like a wand. Then he disappeared down one of the narrow little side streets leading to the centre of town.

I wished I'd thought to ask him his name, and where he lived. But I didn't. Nor did I ever see him again. A few times, I went looking for him, but never found him. I was not a good detective. Or perhaps he was only visiting St-Tropez. I should have asked around. Father Le Coz might have known him. Whether or not he read Plessi's books, who can say? All I know is that I didn't. I still haven't. Nor would I ever listen to them on tape. The idea is preposterous.

✿

Chapter Eight

On the same day the Lyon pilgrims would have returned home from Vatican City and their audience with the Pope, Plessi and I took the coastal train a hundred kilometres west to Marseille. It was an overcast, drizzly day, but warm, and the train was fairly crowded. In our compartment, as far as Toulon, rode a wizened old man in a stained suit and yellow beard, who slept and snored the whole way. How he was able to wake up exactly on the outskirts of Toulon and disembark at the station, I couldn't say. Plessi slept a good deal too, having written ten pages during the night, but at least he didn't snore. Later, in our room at the Mirabeau hotel in Marseille's old port, he snored, but not on the train. His bruises had faded, but still, he wore clip-on sunglasses.

At Toulon, a young man in naval uniform entered our compartment with three small children, a girl and two boys, who took turns whining and going down the corridor to the bathroom. When the coffee lady came by, pushing her cart of packaged cakes and sandwiches, the children successfully lobbied their father for chocolate bars, and while they gorged, were briefly quiet. The older boy, perhaps around seven, spent his time aiming deliberate kicks at Plessi's knapsack, which was on the floor under his bench. The boy's father saw what he was doing, but said nothing, being occupied with his daughter, who complained loudly of feeling sick to her stomach. Sure enough, just before they disembarked at Sanary, she threw up the half-digested contents of her stomach on her father's shiny shoes.

From Sanary to Cassis, which took an hour, we were accompanied by a fat, horsey-looking girl and her grandmother. One of the two had on enough perfume to asphyxiate an army. She smelled like rotting roses. Fortunately, we were in a smoking compartment, so Plessi and I both lit Gauloises and blew smoke at the grandmother, suspecting her as the culprit.

From Cassis to Marseille, a distance of only fifteen kilo-metres, Plessi and I were alone in the compartment. Alone except for the lingering stench of perfume and a sticky mess of chocolate vomit on the floor. Plessi said that ten years pre-viously, he'd spent six months in Marseille, house-sitting the apartment of a journalist friend of his, Martin Bonnieux, who had been posted by *L'Express* to Afghanistan to cover the war. He said he'd used his Marseille time, and the balcony of Martin's apartment on quai des Belges, to write the first draft of a novel, *Papelard*, about a concupiscent priest in the Aquitaine town of Pau, birthplace of King Henri IV. He said it had been a true story, told to him by Martin before he left for Kabul, but that for one reason or another, mostly because it involved altar boys and was horrific, he'd never polished it for publication. He said he'd shown the first draft to Barrage, his agent in Paris, and Barrage had sent it on to Gallimard, who returned it two weeks later, saying that if it were ever published, they, Barrage and Plessi Toussaint would all be incarcerated. There were not enough francs in their entire treasury, they said, to cover the lawsuits that would ensue. Whether it was a true story or not, they didn't care. *L'Express* could publish it as an investigative documentary if they so desired, and Martin Bonnieux could spend two years in a Paris court defending himself if he wished, but Gallimard wanted no part of it. They'd been stung often enough already, and were in no mood to take on the entire Catholic Church. Better, they said, that he should burn the manuscript. Plessi said he hadn't given up on the book, though. He said he was thinking of sending it to Grove Press, Henry Miller's pub-lishers, or perhaps to Barjols, in Holland, who were fearless when it came to smut and intimidated by no one. He said that if he did carry out this idea, and if *Papelard* ever did see the light of day, he might have to come and hide in Canada, in a cabin in the wilds of northern Quebec, and if so, could I arrange this for him? For a fee, of course. For a percentage of the royalties, which would be enormous. Neither of us would ever have to work again. When the ruckus died down, we could buy a château at Aix-en-Provence and live out our lives in opulent comfort. Like Ringo Starr. Like Sean Connery. Like the lady who wrote the Harry Potter books, whose name he'd forgotten.

"J.K. Rowling?" I said.

"That's the one."

When not working on the priest's sordid story during his six months of house-sitting, Plessi had wandered the smelly, swarming streets of Marseille's old port, where Christian soldiers, under Richard the Lionheart, had rallied for the Third Crusade against the Muslims, and where the dread Pneumonic Plague, worse than the Bubonic, having been brought to the Crimea by flea-ridden Mongol soldiers and allowed to spread through Europe, had killed off thousands and made Marseille a ghost town.

As interesting as all this was to Plessi, what caught his attention, as a writer, was the island on the western horizon, on which a fortress-like prison had been built in the early 1500s, known as the Château d'If. The French novelist Alexander Dumas had made the prison famous by having his Count of Monte Cristo escape from it, through a hole in the wall of his cell. Plessi had taken a sightseeing cruise out to the island, had explored the château, had seen the hole through which the Count escaped. The only problem was that Alexander Dumas had concocted the whole thing out of his fertile imagination, so where did the hole come from? In answer to Plessi's question, the tour guide, a vivacious young university student, had said she saw no problem here—that a fictional hole, as described by Dumas, was just as meaningful as a real one. They both existed, and took nothing away from each other. What was more disturbing, she said, and not so easily rationalized, was the actual historical fact that in this same prison, during the Roman Catholic Inquisition, two thousand heretics of Jewish, Islamic and Protestant persuasion were burned or beheaded or otherwise put to death. Papal edicts of the day were clear: toe the line, or else.

Plessi said that all the way back to shore that day, the tour boat had been strangely quiet. As the Château d'If grew hazy behind them, it wasn't the fictional Count of Monte Cristo the passengers were thinking of, but the murdered dissidents, whose only crime had been lack of enlightenment. Crusades, inquisitions, intolerance—things hadn't really changed much since the Middle Ages. Back on the balcony of Martin's apartment, he'd drunk two bottles of wine for dinner, plus one of Armagnac, and awoke next morning with his head through the balustrade, thinking he had a noose around his neck. All night, he'd dreamt of being imprisoned on an island. It was a turning point, he said. After that, he knew his novel about the depraved priest of Pau would never be published. Not in France, anyway.

We took a taxi from the train station, Gare St-Charles, to the hotel Mirabeau, on quai Julien, where we had a large, comfortable room (for short stays, Plessi liked large rooms in good hotels), with a balcony overlooking Marseille's Old Port. The first thing we did, after depositing our knapsacks and flinging open the shutters, was walk along rue de la République to St-Victor hospital, a grey, brooding, fortress-like building with narrow windows, some of which had bars on them. Circumnavigating it, searching for its entrance, the place gave me the creeps. Traffic in the streets was noisy, the air thick with exhaust fumes. I had expected a quiet clinic in the suburbs, surrounded by trees, not a dirty, concrete bastion in the middle of the city. I could well imagine victims of the Black Death gasping out their lives inside. Had I been alone, I would have run back to the hotel and settled my nerves with a few cocktails. Instead, I followed Plessi, who strode along, pretending he knew where he was going. Not until we had entered the main portal, off rue Cézanne, and found ourselves in an airy courtyard full of shrubs did I relax. Though it was late afternoon on a cloudy day, there were a dozen patients, all men, in coats and hats over their pyjamas, sitting on wooden benches. They didn't seem to be talking to each other, just sitting there, looking pale and sickly. Most of them needed a shave. In the foyer, which was crowded with people waiting for something (to be examined? to be excused? to be given medication?), many of them mothers with wailing children, we were told at the information desk that visiting hours were over. A hawk-nosed older nurse in a green smock, after consulting her computer, told Plessi that Monsieur Honoré Velmandois was indeed a patient at St-Victor's, but that unless we were blood relatives, we couldn't see him until ten o'clock next morning. "I'm his brother-in-law," Plessi told her. "And this is his nephew, Guillaume, whose mother, Honoré's sister, is dying of leukemia in Grenoble. We've just come from there, and we must return tonight."

Whether the hawk-nosed nurse believed him or not, I don't know, but she directed us to an elevator at the end of the hall and told us to get off at the sixth floor. Which we did, and after a brief search found Honoré in a room with three other men. I must say, he looked well. There was colour in his cheeks and his eyes were bright. His eyebrows were whiter and bushier than ever and his hair was nicely combed. He was sitting up in bed, reading a newspaper, and was genuinely surprised to see us. He said he'd had a double-bypass operation, during which doctors had taken veins from his leg and transplanted them into his chest as arteries. Plessi thought this highly unlikely, but Honoré insisted it was true. To prove it, he showed us his fresh purple scars. The other men in the room had undergone similar operations, but unlike Honoré, had received three new arteries apiece. Wasn't modern science wonderful? The only trouble was, cigarettes were not allowed, and only two small glasses of wine per day. Every morning, he and his comrades went walking in the courtyard, and every afternoon, hovered over by sprightly nurse-nymphs, dipped their limbs in the basement whirlpool. Once a week, they received a full body massage. Life was good, though the meals were not. In two or three weeks, perhaps a month, he'd be back in Paris, completing his convalescence as an outpatient at Frémicourt, not far from Plessi's apartment on rue

Vaugirard. Speaking of which, was Plessi's invitation still open? Plessi said of course it was, and the timing was perfect, as he planned to be back in Paris by then too. If possible, Honoré should bring a nurse-nymph with him. One who was proficient at full body massages. If she could cook and type as well, so much the better.

"Why the dark glasses?" Honoré asked.

"My eyes are sensitive to light," Plessi said. "As you know, I have nocturnal habits. During the day, I become a bat."

"And the Chirac book?"

"A final chapter, an epilogue, then revisions."

Turning to me, Honoré said, "And your novel?"

"In the germination stage. I'm almost ready to start."

Which made Plessi snort derisively. "He has, how do you call it... cold feet. Yes, when it comes to starting novels, he has cold feet. Ask him instead about Madame Lise Escarène."

Just then the hawk-nosed nurse in the green smock came in with doses of digitalis for all four men. Seeing us, she asked Honoré how his sister was.

"My sister?"

"The one with leukemia. The one at death's door."

"You must be mistaken, madame. I have no sister."

"Then your friend in the sunglasses is a liar, monsieur. He should not be here. And this red-headed person from Grenoble is likely not your nephew. He should not be here either. The rules are to protect you, monsieur. To protect your health."

Taking this as our cue, Plessi and I shook hands with everyone and made our escape, before the hawk-nosed nurse had us evicted. We went down in the elevator, walked through the courtyard, which was now deserted, and out into rue de la République. By then, it was raining, and so Plessi set a brisk pace. As he walked, he sang snatches of *La Marseillaise*, which made people stop and stare at him. He felt justified in singing it, he said, because it was from this very spot, in 1792, that Revolutionaries had marched north to Paris, intent on storming the Bastille and dethroning Louis XVI. As they marched, they sang an old army song, which later became the French national anthem.

The rain let up as we turned into La Canabière, a wide boulevard leading to the Old Port. We followed it down to quai des Belges, where Martin Bonnieux had lived ten years ago. Plessi said he doubted Martin would still be there, but he was. Or rather, his mother was. She was sitting on her second-floor balcony, looking down at us, and when Plessi asked her if she knew Martin Bonnieux, the journalist, she stood up, leaned over the balustrade, and said he was her son. Unfortunately, he wasn't home today. He hadn't been home in quite some time. She thought he might be in Israel. Or Lebanon. Or Afghanistan. She'd wasn't sure. He sent her postcards from all over the world, but she'd lost her glasses. That's why she didn't know for certain where he was. Buenos Aires, perhaps. Did he still work for *L'Express*? No, she didn't think so. She thought he worked for *Le Monde*. Or *Paris Match*. She expected him home for Christmas.

"But Christmas has come and gone, madame."

Vraiment? Really? Well, then, maybe Easter. Sometime. He was probably busy. There was so much going on in the world these days that a journalist was kept busy. Too busy to send his mother postcards in Marseille. Hopefully, he was still alive. Then she sat back down again, under an umbrella, because the rain had returned. It was obvious she wasn't going to invite us up, not with Martin away in Argentina or the Middle East, and so Plessi and I made our way back to the hotel Mirabeau, on quai Julien, with visions of rum grogs dancing in our heads.

"It's too bad Martin wasn't home," Plessi said. "I think you would have liked him."

I'd hoped we might spend two or three days in Marseille, but we didn't. I was hoping to visit Le Château d'If, Fort St-Nicolas, St-Victor's Basilica. I thought we might experience some night life. But we did none of those things. Plessi knew I was disappointed, but he didn't care. He said I could easily come back, after he'd departed for Paris. He said I didn't need him to show me around. If I'd been so interested in Marseille as a Mediterranean city, I should have spent more time there with Dinard and Pascaline months ago, before coming to St-Tropez. He said that Honoré obviously didn't need us, that he was making progress on his own. What was important now was for him to get back to Filles du Soleil and his Chirac book. He did, after all, have a deadline—Easter. Which this year fell at the end of March. And he still had twenty-thousand words of first draft to write. Then revisions, rewriting, and who knew how long that might take? He could not afford to waste time. If I were a serious writer, I would understand this. If I wanted to stay, I was welcome to, but not at his expense. Not at the Hotel Mirabeau, where rooms with balcony overlooking the Old Port cost three-hundred Euros a night, excluding meals, cocktails and taxicabs.

We were not impressed with our expensive dinner in Mirabeau's quai-side dining room. The harbour, packed with pleasure craft and fishing boats, was fine to look at, but the bouillabaisse tasted tinny and was full of bones. The wine was inferior, the pâté sour, the lamb overcooked and tough. Worst were the apples in Calvados for dessert—flabby apples in watery Calvados that tasted like vinegar. Because the meal was so bad, we drank more wine than we should have, and when the waiter approached with the check, Plessi refused to pay it. He said it was an outrage. He said that such food was not fit for German tourists, let alone fellow Frenchmen. In the crowded room, he caused quite a scene. The maître d' came to our table, followed by the hotel manager, followed by the sous-chef. To all of them, Plessi said the same thing—that such food was an insult not only to the palate, but to the pocket book. The sous-chef asked what we'd had, then pursed his lips thoughtfully as Plessi rhymed off the dishes and what was wrong with them. In the end, a new bill was prepared by our waiter, on which the only charge was for two martinis and three bottles of wine. To the waiter, as we were leaving, Plessi said, "Est-ce que vous me connaissez, garçon?" (Do you know who I am?) To which the waiter replied, "Non, monsieur, je n'ai aucune idée. Mais vous avez un accent Parisien." (No, sir, I have no idea, but you have a Parisian accent.)

Later, sitting on our balcony, imbibing the contents of the minibar, Plessi said that since the bad meal hadn't been the waiter's fault, he might have left him a tip, had the man shown any sign of recognition. "My ego and my stomach took a beating tonight, mon gars," he said, unscrewing the cap on his third or fourth miniature Martel. "But what the hell, it's only Marseille, and here in the Moorish provinces, what can one expect? Every race has its barbarians. In Paris, or Bordeau, or Amiens, this would never have happened."

Next morning, after taking Honoré a bag of oranges and walking him twice around the hospital courtyard, we hugged him, wished him health and a strong heart, and caught a taxi to the train station. The rain held off until we were aboard and heading east toward Six-Fours-les-Plages, and then it came down in torrents. Suffering a mild hangover and minor shakes, I was disappointed to learn that the only alcoholic beverage the coffee lady had on her cart was warm beer. So instead I had an espresso, an extra strength Advil, and my next-to-last Gauloise. Out the train window, streaked with rain, flashed glimpses of shoreline. At Toulon, a man, his wife and mongoloid son entered our compartment. The boy, about twelve, clapped his hands at regular intervals and guffawed for no reason. His mother smiled at him benignly, handed him lozenges to suck. His father busied himself with the crossword puzzle in a newspaper. It struck me that this was not an unpleasant place to be, rattling along in a train, heading home to St-Tropez. If only Plessi hadn't been so intent on sleeping. I reasoned he was resting up for his night's work. It's what a serious writer would do. I closed my eyes and thought of Lise Escarène, wondering where she was and what she was doing. I was sorry I hadn't seen the Count of Monte Cristo's cell. The one from which he'd escaped through a fictitious hole in the wall. Beside me, the mongoloid boy was jerking at my sleeve, not to get my attention, but to see what my coat was made of. His father worked doggedly at his crossword puzzle. His mother looked out the window at the rain, humming softly to herself. I wondered if a serious writer, or even an unserious one, could work these elements into a believable story. It seemed unlikely.

Le Relais des Coches, St-Tropez

Chapter Nine

Eventually, Plessi's eye sockets regained their natural colour. Evidence of his defeat at the hands of the two motorcyclists had pretty well faded. He said he sometimes suffered nightmares, though, in which they came back to torment and abuse him. From such dreams, he awoke humiliated. I'm not sure when he first reconciled with Yvette Chanteloup at Crêperie Bretonne, but he did, and began visiting her again on a regular basis. He pretended not to understand why I wouldn't avail myself of her "exceptional services." Was it because I didn't find her svelte and glamorous? She made no claim to be. Nor did she demand those qualities in her customers. Was she not my idea of a sexually-attractive female? If so, I was missing the boat. A romp with a big-bosomed girl would "liberate my creative juices and do me a world of good." From that day on, for reasons which I never understood, he began calling me Carabosse. It became my nickname. "Carabosse," he would say, "are you a fairy? A fucking queer? Yvette would free you from your inhibition and inspire you. It's obviously what you need. Unless you shed your inhibition, you can never be a serious writer."

On the last weekend in February, his Paris agent, Henri Barrage, paid a fleeting visit. He appeared out of nowhere, unannounced, on his way by car from Toulouse to San Remo on the Italian border. He took a room at Hotel Sube, but stayed only one night. The first I knew of his presence was when I discovered him sitting with Plessi at Le Gorille one Saturday afternoon, drinking tea, while Plessi quaffed iced Dubonnet. Until I met him, I'd thought Monsieur Barrage would be a young, hairy, literary-looking fellow. But he wasn't. He was ten years older than Plessi, clean-shaven, nearly bald. He was tanned, healthy-looking, very neatly dressed in sweater, jacket and pressed trousers. He was a non-smoker, drank white wine, swore only when agitated. He could have been a banker, or a real estate agent. His car, a pale-blue Renault, was not the car a successful French literary agent should be driving. As I sat down beside him that day, it struck me that he and Plessi had absolutely nothing in common. They could not have been more dissimilar. Which may have been the secret of their mutually profitable partnership.

"Here is my Canadian protégé, Carabosse," Plessi said by way of introduction. And to me, "This is Monsieur Henri Barrage, my agent, a mean, grasping panderer, who lives off the avails of hard-working writers. You must keep an eye on him at all times. He pretend to be my friend, but in fact is in collusion with my enemies and conspires against me. He thinks I should feel indebted to him. He cannot accept the fact that I owe him absolutely nothing."

To my surprise, Henri Barrage didn't laugh at this. He was not the laughing kind. Nor was he at all interested in me, or in what I'd written, or hoped to write. What he was interested in was Plessi's forthcoming book, tentatively entitled, *Le Fétish*. He asked to see the manuscript. He said he could devote an afternoon and evening to it. But Plessi said no, it would be bad luck to show it to anyone at this stage. Like a mother lark who rejects her hatchlings if they've been touched by human hands. He assured Monsieur Barrage it was nearing completion, in first draft. "You know I'm a man of my word," he said. "You know, Henri, how hard I work. Have I ever let you down?"

"Yes," Henri said. "Several times."

"Once or twice, perhaps. But never without cause."

"My concern, Plessi, is that the book must be in Gallimard's hands a month from tomorrow. Not in first, second or third draft, but in final draft, ready for the editors."

"My books, Henri, as you very well know, require no editing. Or very little."

"I wish that were true. It takes a week to correct the spelling mistakes. Another week to check facts. Another week to change the names of living people. Even so, they sue us. Profits are eaten up by legal fees. And for every month you're late on delivery, we lose a percentage of our royalties. It's in the contract."

Plessi lit a Gauloise, signalled Marius for refills. "Do you detect, Carabosse, what I'm up against? You see how he refers to it as *our* royalties? You see why agents are the scum of the earth, why authors like me are driven to suicide? My advice to you—forget about becoming a writer. Sell magazines door to door. Learn a trade. Anything."

As I recall, we spent the rest of the afternoon at Le Gorille, and most of the evening too. Plessi and I got mellow on Dubonnet. Monsieur Barrage drank tea and nibbled Madeira cakes, which he insisted were called *madeleines*—the same cookies Marcel Proust dips into his tea in *A La Recherche du Temps Perdu*. Plessi tried to tell him that Madeira cakes weren't *madeleines* at all, but something quite different, and as they argued back and forth, voices rising, I realized that there was genuine animosity between them. I don't know why this should have surprised me, but it did. Theirs appeared to be a love-hate relationship, and I wondered whether all successful writers resented their agents, and vice versa. With Plessi Toussaint and Henri Barrage, distrust and dislike seemed to bubble beneath the surface. I remember thinking it wouldn't take much for them to start trading insults, and after that, trading punches. Or perhaps the iced Dubonnet was making me misjudge.

As evening fell, Le Gorille became crowded. The first transients of the season seemed to have arrived, coming in by car from Aubagne and Ste-Maxime. Two or three sail-boats docked. Marius and a new waiter, Antoine, were scampering from table to table, bringing drinks and oysters and baskets of shrimp. We ourselves ordered a platter of sea bass, which we ate with our fingers, and a carafe of chilled Vougeot. Henri Barrage barely sipped his wine, and seemed content to nibble bread and radishes, while Plessi and I made pigs of ourselves. We sucked grease off our fingertips, belched, broke wind, shouted pleasantries at nearby tables, and as we did so, I sensed that Plessi was trying to embarrass his agent, make him feel like an intruder. But again, I may have been wrong. Once, when Plessi excused himself and went indoors to the washroom, Monsieur Barrage said to me, "My purpose in coming here, my duty, if you will, is to spur him on. To make sure he knows the deadline is approaching. Sometimes he can be irresponsible. With him, one never knows until one sees the manuscript how many dignitaries he's defamed, how many libel suits to anticipate. This is not an easy business, handling temperamental, egotistical authors, who write what they please without regard for public taste or legal matters."

I thought he sounded needlessly defensive. He certainly didn't need to justify himself to me. I said I knew very well how difficult and unpredictable Plessi could be, but that maybe that's what made him a good writer. "I think your fears about the deadline are groundless, Monsieur Barrage. I know that Plessi has been diligent since well before Christmas, putting in long hours at his word processor, locked in his room every night."

Monsieur Barrage shrugged. "Well, possibly. Yet you say he took time off to have a fist fight and go to Marseille to see a friend. And how do you know what he does in his room? He has the reputation of never letting anyone in while he's working. You see, Monsieur Carabosse, or whatever the hell your name is, I've been through this before with Plessi Toussaint. With all his books—*Magnéto, Crédillon, Condamné, Jocrisse*— all of them. And it's always been a struggle. I need time to prepare the publisher and hire lawyers. So don't tell me my fears are groundless. I need no advice from novices. I've known Plessi Toussaint a damn sight longer than you, and I assure you, he's neither diligent nor trustworthy. Like most authors, forgive my saying so, he's a vain, impractical braggart. Also a bullshit artist. Don't be taken in by him. If it weren't for me, he'd be a pauper. Or in prison. Or assassinated."

This indeed was food for thought. "I assume you've never been a writer yourself, Monsieur Barrage?"

He dipped another Madeira cake in his tea, sucked the soggy end, savoured it. "Good heavens, no. I could never lock myself in a room for months on end, just to write a book that will probably be rejected anyway. What a waste of time. I have better things to do. Nor is my sense of self-worth so low that it needs reassurance. Life is short. I never spend more than ten minutes writing a letter. Which is why I have a secretary, who happens to be my eldest daughter. If I wanted to, I could probably be a very good editor. But may I tell you something? What I do best is judge the saleability of manuscripts. I've never been wrong yet. When I approach a publisher with a client's work, they know I'm not wasting their time. They know they can trust me. Which is why I rarely have difficulty placing a book. Which is why Plessi Toussaint, despite what he says, needs me more than I need him. Which is why my fee is twenty per cent, and why writers are happy to pay it. I'm that good. Probably the best."

Next morning, when I went down to Le Gorille for breakfast, the sun was shining and it really did feel like spring. There was a warm wind blowing in off the Mediterranean, making sailboats' rigging rattle. Fishing sloops were busy, the gulls more boisterous than usual. As for me, I felt thick-headed and ill. My hands shook. The sun was too bright, the wind too strong. I needed sunglasses to combat the glare. People's voices were too loud. I didn't remember drinking more than usual the night before, but must have. My excuse was that pompous Henri Barrage was a pain in the ass. I mentioned this to Plessi, and he agreed. "Didn't I tell you long ago, mon gars, that he was, how do call it? an arrogant prick? Now you know."

We had rum grogs with our omelets, and good strong coffee, and after two Gauloises I felt better. My hands settled down, my vision cleared. Plessi said he'd put in a good night of writing, had been forced to discard hardly anything in the harsh light of day. Which was probably a sign that the end of the book was in sight. Which in turn distressed him, because it meant he had limited time left to instruct me on how to be a serious writer. How to overcome my inertia and settle down to hard work, as he did. "If only I could unlock your brain,

mon gars. Find a way to unshackle you. I've tried everything.
I've made suggestion. But so far I've failed. Which is not to
say that all is lost. There is still time. If I succeed in, how do
you say it? getting your ass in gear, someday you'll thank me."

"Is that your mission statement?"

"What is this, mission statement?"

"Your plan. What you intend to accomplish."

"Yes, that is my mission statement."

He said he'd consumed just enough wine at dinner to get
him through the night, like a jazz musician fuelling up on
cocaine before a concert. He asked me if I'd ever tried
cocaine, and I said no. He said he had, one New Year's Eve at
the Moulin Rouge in Montmartre, watching the Nude Bul-
garian Review. Talk about a chorus line. Toulouse-Lautrec
would have turned over in his grave. Great bouncing mam-
maries. Thickets of brush an elephant could hide in.
Unshaved armpits. The stage had trembled. He said he had-
n't enjoyed the drug, because although he felt euphoric, it had
scrambled his brains and made him light-headed. Had I ever
tried hashish or marijuana? Yes, I said, a few times. As recently as last fall, on the train from Marseille with Dinard and
Pascaline. We'd smoked pipefuls of poor quality hashish
which they'd obtained in Tarascon. It had made us giggle
uncontrollably. Unfortunately, when the hashish was gone,
they'd asked me for two-hundred dollars to cover the cost of
my share. Which was enough to make me stop giggling. At
one time, Plessi said, in Auxerre, where he'd lived with a
woman whose son was a dealer, he'd smoked a lot of marijuana, but found that it ruined his concentration and made him
a second-class writer. Affected his memory. Booze, he said,
especially red wine from Médoc, taken in just the right
amount, was the best stimulant of all, with rum grogs at the
end of the night as a reward for good work. Did I not agree?
I certainly did.

After waiting till ten o'clock for Henri Barrage, we
walked over to the Hotel Sube and were told by the desk clerk
that he had checked out at dawn and would be halfway to

Nice by now. Feeling slighted, and perhaps envious, Plessi and I went back to Le Gorille and finished our breakfast.

I believe it was that same day, or possibly the next, that I met Yvette Chanteloup's cousin, Iseult. At first, I thought her last name was also Chanteloup, until I discovered that she was Yvette's cousin on her mother's side, and that her last name was Plonevez. Her father, Graslin, owns a large poultry farm in Bourg-en-Bresse, of which her brother, Jean-Bart, is manager. Their specialty is chickens with blue feet, which are considered a gastronomic delicacy in the region. Iseult's mother, Angéline, Yvette's aunt, with a history of mental illness, is a self-proclaimed authority on Gothic architecture and gives lectures to sparse audiences in the flamboyant Eglise de Brou. I've been invited to go up to Bourg-en-Bresse when I leave here, and may just do it. Iseult's family sounds fascinating. She claims to be directly descended from Philibert le Beau, Duke of Savoy. Although Plessi was skeptical when he heard this, I saw no reason to doubt it.

Iseult is a large girl, like her cousin, and, if anything, more outgoing. She wears glasses, has fair hair, exudes nonchalance. Her favourite apparel consists of wide-brimmed hats and loose-fitting blouses covered with geometric designs. She is not the least bit self-conscious about her size. She speaks English and German fluently, having worked as an au pair girl in Saarbrucken and St. Peter Port. Plessi once told me he was under the impression she'd been married to the curator of a bird sanctuary in Villar-les-Dombes. She may have been. I never asked her. When I met her, she wore no rings, and referred to herself as *une fille non mariée*.

Plessi came to my room late one afternoon, while I was sitting at the window with the shutters open, wondering what to do with myself, and said that I should put on a clean shirt and go with him to meet Yvette Chanteloup's cousin, Iseult. She was in town for a few days, helping out at Crêperie Bretonne, as she did two or three times a year, and was staying with Yvette at her apartment on rue Matisse. This, he said, would be a social call, not a business call (Yvette did not receive clients at her apartment anymore—the concierge forbade it), and such invitations were not extended to just anyone. Yvette was a respectable, educated girl from a good family, who, had she wanted to, could have become a secretary, a nurse, or a school teacher. I should feel honoured. I should put on a few drops of cologne.

On the way to rue Matisse, we stopped in at La Frégate, on rue de le Renaissance, for a Pernod. I could tell by the way he smoked that Plessi was excited. Walking behind him, I had to hurry to keep up. I don't know whether he'd ever been to Yvette's apartment before, but I doubt it. The thing I remember is its forest-green walls. That and the presence of the two hefty women, who, until they began shedding their clothes, seemed to fill the premises. There were wicker chairs, couches covered in red cloth, paintings of swamp flowers, done by Yvette. There was a plaster bust of the Greek historian, Diodorus Siculus, known for his compendium of the world in forty volumes (according to Yvette) on a shelf beside the door. Within minutes, I felt at ease. There was something about the place, something relaxed and homey. It might have been the incense smouldering in a corner. Or the jungle-green walls. Or the soft glow of lamps. We had several drinks—vodka martinis, as I recall—and Yvette put on a CD of Celine Dion, singing in French.

To this day, I don't know if Plessi knew what to expect. If he did, he kept it from me. Mind you, it's possible he engineered the whole event. Despairing of ever getting me to indulge myself at Crêperie Bretonne, he might have resorted to this underhanded charade. It might have been a challenge to him—seeing if he could corrupt me, break my virginal resolve. I don't know. As he'd said, he didn't have much time left. Only until Easter.

After our third or fourth drink, Yvette and Iseult got up and began dancing with each other. Then they pulled Plessi to his feet and danced with him. Then they pulled me up, and we all danced together. Not loudly or vigorously, but quietly, suggestively. We had more drinks, and the girls began shedding outer garments. Iseult took off her hat and blouse. Yvette removed her skirt. I remember thinking I'd never seen such thighs. Tree-trunk thighs. Thighs twice the thickness of Lise Escarène's. Thighs that could injure a man if he weren't careful. Do him permanent damage. And yet, as we danced, these same thighs became oddly provocative. I can't explain it. Plessi probably could. It may have been what he'd meant by Yvette's "exceptional services." Dancing with Iseult, I felt strangely buoyant, as though I were floating. She pressed me in tightly against her, so that I could feel the bulge of her stomach. She took control. It was like sinking into a soft, warm comforter. Her breasts were spongy pillows. There was something maternal about it. Something sisterly. Protective, yet liberating. Cares evaporated. Inhibitions vanished. We danced, kissed, danced some more. Then we stopped for a drink and the girls stripped down to their underwear. Plessi, I noticed, had his shirt and trousers off. I'd never seen his hairy legs before, his hairy back, his hairy chest. He still had his glasses on, his socks, his brown hat. It was all I could do to keep from laughing. I knew now why he'd told me to put on cologne, although in that haze of incense smoke, the cologne was likely redundant. Celine Dion kept singing, we kept dancing. Iseult said, "You dance well, Carabosse. Have you taken lessons?"

"Yes," I said. "But not in dancing."

I'm not sure when I realized that Plessi and Yvette were not in the room. It may have been when Iseult took off the rest of her clothes and urged me to do the same. When I looked around, I saw that we were alone. From the adjoining bedroom came sounds of lewd laughter. Iseult and I danced naked for a while, circling slowly, then collapsed gently on the red sofa. Never had intimate physicality been so effort-less, so exciting. I remember Iseult telling me to take it easy. To leave things to her. Which I was happy to do. I also remember understanding, finally, in a blinding flash, what Plessi had been trying to tell me. He was, I suddenly realized,

a brilliant man. What insight! What genius. No wonder he
wrote best-selling books. If he wanted to, he could solve the
riddle of the Sphinx. Of the Mona Lisa. Of Adam and Eve.
Of Sodom and Gomorrah.

In the next room, I could hear him shouting. Or he
might have been begging for a second helping of jam tarts.
Maybe he was only laughing. I don't know. I heard him call
out Yvette's name. Soon, I was doing some laughing and begging of my own. It might have been the time to ask Iseult if
her ex-husband was really the curator of a bird sanctuary in
Villar-les-Dombes.

When I woke up, I had no idea how long I'd been asleep.
It could have been morning, it could have been night. I suspect it was like being born. I was lying naked on the red
couch, my head in Iseult's lap, and she was smoking a cigarette. Celine Dion was still singing. I could hear Plessi and
Yvette singing along with her, harmonizing. They sounded
like professionals.

"Carabosse," Iseult said, seeing me awake, running her
fingers through my hair, "you're a wild man. Plessi Toussaint
was right about you. You're suppressed, like a volcano."

"Not any more," I said, accepting the Gauloise she stuck
between my lips.

The four of us went to Le Relais des Coches for bowls of
matelote at midnight. I was still in a daze, stupefied, mum-
mified, but relaxed and happy. Never had I experienced such
a feeling of well-being. My three friends were clever, scintil-
lating. The Côtes du Rhône was incredibly delicious, the fish
stew as succulent as I'd ever tasted. There was a full moon, a
mild onshore breeze. The night was magical. Down the street,
someone was playing melancholy music on a harmonica.
Auguste, our waiter, poured our wine and lit our cigarettes,
which was something Marius had seldom done at Le Gorille.

At two o'clock in the morning, ours was the only table
still occupied. Plessi, seeing Auguste yawning, said it was time
to call it a night. He had ten pages to write before sunup.

Yvette said she had to be at Crêperie Bretonne in five hours, when the first pancake customers would appear for breakfast. Iseult said she needed to be up early to catch the north-bound train to Grenoble, Lyon and Bourg-en-Bresse, where a hen-house full of blue-footed chickens and a crazy mother awaited her. Like everyone else, she had commitments.

"And you, Carabosse," she said, holding my hand, ruffling my hair. "Where do you need to go?"

I kissed her on the lips. Not to thank her, or express my gratitude, but because it was two o'clock in the morning and she was quite beautiful. Her wide-brimmed hat was at a jaunty angle. "I need to go to bed, over there, across the street, at Filles du Soleil. I may sleep for two days."

"Les Filles du Soleil," she said. "Daughters of the Sun. It's what my cousin Yvette and I used to be called, when we were younger and thinner. My mother called us that. Daughters of the sun. We never knew why, but we liked it. Now we have a hotel named after us in St-Tropez. We're famous."

"It's not a hotel," I said.

"No?"

"It's a rooming house. Une maison de rapport."

"Well, Monsieur Carabosse, be thankful it's not une maison de fous. A madhouse."

Plessi stood up, drained his glass, kissed both girls' cheeks. It seemed to me a rather formal gesture, after the kind of night we'd had. "But it is," he said. "That's exactly what it is. A fucking madhouse. I've always said that. A house of madmen pretending to be writers."

❖

Iseult Plonevez

La Frégate, St-Tropez

Oddly enough, I slept poorly that night. My mind kept going in circles. Halfway between dream and reality, I wondered what being married to the curator of a bird sanctuary in remote Villars-les-Dombes would be like. Would one go slowly insane? Or quickly insane? Would one feel cut off from mainstream society? Would one escape to Lyon, Dijon, Grenoble, as often as one could? What if one had a retarded son or daughter? Would one feel burdened and contemplate murder? Suicide? Would there be headlines in the tabloids? "Mad wife of bird custodian allegedly kills child, husband, wounds self." Tormented by these images, I rose at first light and began scratching thoughts down on paper. I opened the shutters wide, felt the fresh, cool air of a Mediterranean morning. I had no electric kettle, so couldn't brew tea, but I smoked several Gauloises and let my thoughts flow. So intent was I on my work that I failed to notice the sun come up. I remember looking out and seeing it in the sky, and children on their way to school, and Plessi Toussaint sitting by himself at Le Gorille, reading a newspaper.

At breakfast, I didn't tell him I'd hurdled some kind of barrier and felt ready to start a novel. Still, he must have sensed something, because he kept saying, "Carabosse, I do believe last night have changed you. You look different this morning. What did you think of Iseult Plonevez, daughter of a chicken farmer?"

"I liked her."

"You enjoyed yourself?"

"I did."

"I thought you would. It's too bad she left this morning on the train to Grenoble. You might have married with her. C'est dommage."

"Or maybe it's just as well."

"You should have gone with her to see her father's rare blue-legged chickens."

"She told me I was welcome to visit her anytime I happened to be in Bourg-en-Bresse."

"That prove she likes you, mon gars. Will you go?"

"I might. Someday."

"It would make her happy. She's had the difficult life."

I waited for him to tell me why, but he didn't. He said he'd worked hard during the night, had made progress with his Chirac book. He said he'd dealt with two nefarious characters, Bernard Arnault and Claude Lavigne, was glad to be rid of them, because now it would be smooth sailing to the end. I gathered they were members of the Assemblée Nationale, but the names meant nothing to me.

He reminded me again that he'd soon be leaving St-Tropez and going back to Paris with his manuscript and its computer disk. He said that if I were ever in Paris, I should look him up, but not to expect him to sit around waiting for me. He had places to visit, acquaintances to renew. He'd heard rumours that Gallimard wanted him to spend the summer on the island of Guernsey, where Victor Hugo had written *Les Misérables* in a house overlooking St. Peter Port, while enjoying the ministrations of his recently widowed housekeeper. Surely here were possibilities for a book. Also, Gallimard's editor-in-chief, a man named Sénéquier, had said he thought it would be prudent if Plessi was out of the country when his Chirac exposé was launched. Oh, and Plessi had almost forgotten to tell me—he'd received a letter from Honoré Velmandois, who was back in Paris recuperating, not at Frémicourt, as expected, but at Clinique Sainte-Isabelle, in the Neuilly suburbs, near the Bois de Boulogne, where he shared a vine-covered house with two matronly physiotherapists. It was, he said, a perfect arrangement, and Plessi was welcome to visit anytime, as was his Canadian friend, whose name, at the moment, Honoré had forgotten. In case Plessi was interested, Scott Fitzgerald's wife, Zelda, had spent time at Clinique Sainte-Isabelle, in the psychiatric ward, before the war.

Plessi said he hated farewells, might leave St-Tropez without saying *arrivederci*. If he did, I was not to take it personally. One morning, I'd be sitting at Le Gorille waiting for him, but he'd be gone. I must not think badly of him for doing this. It was his way. He would be relieved, he said, to deliver the Chirac book to Henri Barrage on Good Friday, or Easter Sunday at the latest, and tell him what a distrustful prick he was for doubting his best author. He said he was anxious to be back in Paris, not just because the cost of living in St-Tropez would skyrocket April 1st, as it always did, but because Paris was where his roots were. "It's my home," he said. "It's where my soul resides. If I'm absent too long, I'll fall ill and die. Or lose my mental capacity, as did Guy de Maupassant, our hero. I'm not accustomed to all this Mediterranean sunshine. As you know, I work best in the dark, and Paris, for most of the year, is a dark city, with clouds on the rooftops. I believe its latitude is the same as your northern Ontario. You would know better than I."

"But you once told me you weren't born in Paris."

"No one is ever born in Paris, Carabosse. They're born in Tours, or Nantes, or some Alsatian village. But Paris is where you go to live. It becomes your home. When you're away for any length of time, you become despondent and must return, as you yourself must return to the frozen steppes of Canada. It's where you belong and feel comfortable. Unless you're strong enough to be an immigrant, and very few people are. They either go home to die, or dream of going home to die, or end up killing themselves, which amounts to the same thing."

We sat there in the morning sun, drinking coffee, smoking cigarettes. I didn't know if anything he'd said made sense, but I knew I'd miss the sound of his voice when he left. I wanted him to keep talking. I debated telling him I thought I was on the verge of breaking out of my literary impasse, but I didn't. He may have read my mind, because he said, "I'm sorry, Carabosse, that I haven't inspired you to write something. I swear to God, I tried. Maybe in my absence, inspiration will come to you. I hope so. Otherwise, you've wasted half a year, and who can afford to do that? You know, mon gars, that life is a tragedy. Never forget. As long as you remember, you can be a serious writer. Think of Proust, Camus, Stendhal, de Maupassant. Or, in desperation, as a last resort, think of me."

That day, after he went up to bed, instead of prowling the waterfront and drinking rum grogs, I went to my room. Despite trembling fingers and a headache, I wrote out four pages of my bourgeoning novel in longhand. It wasn't much (on a good night, Plessi could do ten times that), but it was a start. I tried to recall the name of the shop on rue Sibilli where Plessi had rented his Bandol word processor, but couldn't. Perhaps, I thought, when he's finished with his, I could borrow it. The only problem would be that he'd ask why, and I preferred not to say. And so next morning I walked the length of rue Sibilli, found the computer store, and after swearing the clerk to secrecy, rented a Bandol word processor of my own.

Plessi worked hard most of March, and so did I. The only difference was that while he started work after supper and wrote till dawn, I seldom lasted past midnight. I didn't have the stamina. Not at first. Nor could I figure out the correct dose of energizer. If I drank more than three rum grogs and four glasses of wine at dinner, I would doze off in mid-sentence. If I drank less than that, my hands shook and I couldn't sit still. I tried spiking my morning coffee with Pernod, which fuelled me till noon, but unless I consumed at least a carafe of wine at lunch, my brain went catatonic. There were days when I thought the walls of my room were closing in on me. I saw caterpillars on the floor, bats hanging from the ceiling. Faces stared at me through the shutters, women's voices called for help from among the tethered sailboats. Several times a day I went downstairs, crossed the street, and stood on the sea wall, listening. All I heard were radios blaring, children calling. Marius, at Le Gorille, would see me,

call out to me, ask what I was doing. I would go back inside
Filles du Soleil, return to my room, hammer away at the
word processor. Slowly, painfully, the story of Iseult (you
didn't have to be a brain surgeon to figure out that's who my
heroine was) took shape. Her husband's name was Hoche
and his spooky bird refuge was a horrid, isolated place, full
of unhatched eggs and deformed vultures in cages. Iseult,
whose name in the story was Livie, became monstrous too.
Her mentally challenged son, Porcelet, totally dependent on
her but ignored by his reclusive father, became a millstone
around her neck. She longed to escape both husband and
son, contemplated poisoning one, drowning the other. The
three of them lived alone in a blockhouse surrounded by
squawking birds and guano. The noise and stench were awe-
some. They had no friends, no visitors. Nor was there any
meaning to their lives. And yet, cruelly, Livie alone seemed
dissatisfied. She longed for communication, but her husband
never spoke and her son made no sense. They spent every
Christmas alone, every Easter, every Bastille Day, while other
families congregated and celebrated. Some nights, Livie
would go out among the pens and screech like a peacock.
Other days, she'd make not a sound. On rare occasions, scientists would show up, and she would hide in the house with
her drooling son, ashamed of him, ashamed of herself. It was
after one of these scientific visits, when she'd looked out the
window and seen a bearded ornithologist, and he'd seen her,
and had waved, and smiled, that she decided she would rid
herself once and for all of Porcelet and Hoche and start a
new life. Who could blame her? And if she made it look acci-
dental, who would know? She'd find a nice, normal family,
who spent Christmas and Epiphany together, who went to
church, exchanged gifts. She'd seen such families on television. Oddly, her husband never watched television and her
son didn't understand it. He had no idea where the pictures
were coming from, even after she explained it to him. One
day, unattended for five minutes, he'd taken a hammer and
smashed the set open, trying to locate the people. There had

been white powder and broken glass everywhere, and Porcelet had hooted like a monkey.

And that's where I was, on page 112 of *Birdman's Wife*, when Plessi left St-Tropez. It was Palm Sunday. Just as he'd warned, he left without a word of goodbye. No letter, no note. I sat and waited for him all morning at Le Gorille, sipped two rum grogs on an empty stomach, spoke sharply to Marius when he hovered at my elbow. By ten o'clock, I had a premonition. I could have asked Marius, but didn't. Anyway, he was ignoring me, had turned me over to Antoine. I went across the street to Filles du Soleil, climbed the stairs, banged on Plessi's unlocked door. Of course, there was no answer. I opened it, saw that the room was empty, closed it again. I went down to the apartment of Monsieur Nemours, the concierge of Filles du Soleil, asked where Plessi Toussaint was. "Ah, monsieur," Nemours said, "il est parti pour Paris. Il ne revient pas." He's left for Paris. He's not returning.

Just as I thought. Just as I'd feared.

I went back to Le Gorille, ordered a third rum grog from Antoine, sat by myself in the sun, watching tables fill up with strangers. I sat there till noon, drinking rum grogs as fast as Antoine brought them. After a lunch of quiche and crépinettes, I went home to bed, though apparently not directly. Next day, when I stopped in for an emergency martini, Antoine told me I had fallen headfirst into the shrubbery on the boulevard, and that he himself, not Marius, after watching me regurgitate my lunch, had helped me across the street and upstairs to my room. For which I thanked him and left a large tip.

Next day, or it might have been two or three days later, having written not a word past page 112 of *Birdman's Wife*, I walked down the street to Crêperie Bretonne. As it was still early, Yvette Chanteloup was sitting alone at a table under the awning. She was wearing a sweater over her apron, drinking a cup of coffee. When she saw me, she glanced away.

"Mademoiselle," I said, "I assume you know that Plessi Toussaint has returned to Paris. He's no longer in St-Tropez."

Still avoiding eye contact, Yvette folded her ample arms across her chest. "What are you, le crieur public?" The town crier?

"No, I just wondered if you knew that Plessi's gone."

"Of course I knew. Do I look stupid?"

I chalked her belligerence up to melancholy. Or lack of business. She'd lost a paying customer. It occurred to me that we'd never had a conversation. "As a former sunshine girl, you don't look happy."

"A former what?"

"Sunshine girl. Fille du soleil. I seem to recall your cousin Iseult saying that the two of you, when you were young, were known as daughters of the sun. Remember?"

"No, I don't remember. It's true, but I don't remember. She must have been high on herbs."

"I think we were all high on herbs. I know I was."

"Speak for yourself."

"I was wondering if Plessi told you he was leaving."

"Of course he told me. He bring me a silver necklace."

"How nice. He never said a word to me."

"Why should he?"

"I thought we were friends."

"Plessi Toussaint have no friends. Only enemies."

If she had asked me to, I'd have sat down, bought a cup of coffee, ordered a plate of waffles. But she didn't. "Did he leave a message? Did he mention me?"

"What kind of imbécile are you?"

So I walked away, back up the street toward Le Gorille. But then I thought, who the hell does she think she is, talking to me like that? I retraced my steps, stood in front of her. "You may not understand it, Mademoiselle Chanteloup, but I liked him. I respected him. I spent as much time with him as you did, maybe more. I went to Marseille with him. When he was in a bad mood, I was there for him to be pissed off at. He gave me pointers on writing."

"He should have given you a pointer in your head. I know about you, P 1ètre. He ask you a hundred times to come see me, and you don't. You walk around with your nose in the hair and a stick up your ass. You are no friend of Plessi Toussaint."

"My name's not Piètre."

She looked puzzled, amused. I thought I detected the flicker of a smile. "I never say it is. I call you a piece of shit. You should learn the language."

"Your cousin Iseult told me my French was fine."

"She also stuff her husband full of schnapps and let the pigs eat him."

At least I think that's what she said. I'm not sure. Her first clients of the day were coming down the street, American tourists. I said, "Au revoir, fille du soleil," but by then she was inside the crêperie and may not have heard me.

I missed Easter. It came and went unnoticed. On Good Friday, waking from a sweaty dream in which I'd been in Malaga, watching Holy Week processions, I went to my window, opened the shutters and imagined I saw a crucified, papier-mâché Jesus riding by on a float. I could have sworn I heard trumpets too. It took a few moments to realize I was in St-Tropez, not Malaga. Fortunately, after I'd blinked a few times, Jesus and his float disappeared and the harbour full of sailboats swam into focus.

After that, I pretty much lost track of days and nights. I sat at my word processor hour after hour, staring out the window at the St-Tropez lighthouse. When it flashed, I guessed it was dark out. When it stopped flashing, I assumed the sun was up and stumbled over to Le Gorille for a liquid breakfast. Marius, clairvoyant Marius, sensing my restlessness, insisted I pay my tab promptly, where before he'd been in no rush. He must have known my money was running out. He said he would understand if I departed suddenly for home—it was the rainiest spring he could ever remember. Boat owners who had come to prepare their craft for summer sat morosely ashore, waiting for the fog to lift. The first cruise ship of the season, the *Marco Polo*, steamed by one evening at sunset, bound, I suppose, for Genoa. Marius said he hoped she would anchor and send tourists ashore, but she didn't.

Next morning he did something he'd never done before. Without saying anything, he placed a copy of *Le Monde* on my table, beside my rum grog, and walked quickly away. When I turned the paper over, there was Plessi Toussaint's face on the front page. Until I read the headline, I thought maybe he'd won another prize. Or that Gallimard was preparing readers for the advent of his new book, *Le Fétish*. But that wasn't it at all. That's not why his picture was on the front page of *Le Monde*. It was there because he was dead.

I put the newspaper down, picked it up, put it down again. If my hands had been trembling before, they now shook with palsy. My first reaction was denial. Disbelief. The fools had pulled a colossal boner. It happened all the time. Wrong person, wrong story. A retraction would be forthcoming. I contemplated standing up on my chair and telling people to ignore the sensational, attention-grabbing headlines. You can't believe half what you read in the western press these days. But I didn't. I sat as still as possible, waiting for my breath to come back and my hands to quiet. I looked around for Marius, saw him standing at the far end of the bar. I finished off my rum grog, signalled him for a refill. Strangely, he pretended not to notice me. Or perhaps he really didn't. He may have been looking past me, or through me, thinking his own thoughts. I curbed an impulse to rise and demand that he tell me what the hell had happened, what kind of sick joke this was. Then I picked up the newspaper again.

It said that Plessi Toussaint, one of France's foremost novelists and *cancanniers*—tattlers—had drowned in the Seine, in Paris. His lifeless body had been found washed ashore on Ile St-Louis, so speculation by authorities was that he had fallen, jumped or been pushed off Pont de Sully. Or if not that, then off quai St-Bernard on the Left Bank, or quai

Henri IV, on the right. No one knew for certain. There were barges and bateaux-mouches tied up on quai St-Bernard, from which he might have entered the river. Police were still investigating. They intended to interview witnesses, some of whom had told the Préfecture they'd seen people scuffling on Pont de Sully the night before. The chief inspector of La Sûreté, Monsieur Forges-Gemmail, couldn't rule out the possibility that Plessi Toussaint had fallen or been thrown in the water upstream and drifted down. Or he might have been jettisoned from a passing pleasure craft. Who could say? At the moment, the drowning was being considered fortuitous. According to a spokesman at Gallimard, Monsieur Toussaint's books, such as *Condamné*, *Jocrisse*, *Magnéto* and *Crédillon*, had created controversy. Their author was a controversial man, against whom people were known to have grudges. Regrettably, his new book, *Le Fétish*, set in Paris and Chartres, the manuscript of which had just come into their hands via Monsieur Toussaint's agent, Henri Barrage, would now need to be published posthumously. It was not yet known whether there was any connection between the contents of *Le Fétish* and Plessi Toussaint's untimely demise. A reliable source at the editorial offices of Gallimard had informed *Le Monde* that in *Le Fétish*, national and municipal politics were entangled.

When I looked up, Marius had placed a fresh rum grog at my elbow and emptied my ashtray. By the time I'd read the front page a second time, I'd made some decisions. One was not to go to Paris for the funeral. What would be the point? Another was to vacate Filles du Soleil as soon as possible. I could not bear the thought of living there, now that Plessi was dead. Besides, it was time to leave St-Tropez. There was nothing for me now. Less than nothing. My money was almost gone, my novel abandoned. Or if not abandoned, suspended. I saw no purpose in continuing it. Still, I'd take it with me wherever I went, just in case. There might be long, empty nights when I could add to it. Perhaps, after putting Plessi's memory to rest, I'd be sparked with fresh inspiration. In the meantime, before returning the rented word processor, I'd hammer out some thoughts and impressions of the winter just past. In fact, if necessary, I'd take paper and pencil down to Le Gorille and pretend to be Hemingway or Fitzgerald.

What I wanted to do, what I had an impulsive urge to do, was catch the train to Bourg-en-Bresse and look for Iseult Plonevez. I couldn't have said why, but it seemed necessary, almost urgent. Truthfully, I longed for her, like a patient longs for a night nurse, like a lonely person longs for a companion. Loneliness was something I'd never had to contend with before, but now it loomed like a spectre. I felt no desire to go looking for Honoré Velmandois in Paris, or for Lise Escarène in Agay. Nor did I feel like returning home. Something, some force stronger than reason, ill-advised or not, was pulling me north to the valley of the Saône, where chickens with blue feet lived on a farm with Iseult Plonevez, who may or may not have fed her husband to the pigs. She was, moreover, the muse and heroine of my aborted novel, *Birdman's Wife*. Perhaps all I needed was to see this remote bird sanctuary, this Parc des Oiseaux, at Villars-les-Dombes. Down deep, I felt sure that Plessi, if he were here, would urge me to go. I could hear him saying, "Do it, mon gars. Do it. Your muse awaits you, and don't forget, she did invite you. The daughter of the sun invite you. Get on the train and go. If you don't, you'll never be a serious writer."

I summoned Marius, who approached slowly, his face longer than I'd ever seen it. Looking at him, I wondered just how sincere his apparent grief really was. I asked him if he'd ever heard of a town in the eastern province of Franche-Comté, not far from the Swiss border, called Bourg-en-Bresse. He said he had, Of course he had. He knew people living in the region. He'd been to Bourg-en-Bresse as an adolescent, to visit his dying grandmother. They'd taken the train from Dijon, had stayed at a hotel called Le Terminus, right next to the station. They'd eaten their meals outdoors

on the terrace, the specialty of the house being poulet rôti
aux pattes bleues—roast blue-footed chicken. Did he think
Le Terminus was still there? He didn't see why not. If I
walked over to the St-Tropez train depot and asked, they
could probably tell me.

Umberto

Monsieur Nemours

Epilogue

❂

With my 2nd class train ticket to Bourg-en-Bresse in my pocket and *Le Monde* in my hand, I walked down the street to Crêperie Bretonne with the intention of bidding Yvette adieu. When I arrived, she said she'd heard the news on the radio, but hadn't read the paper. She was sad, distracted, but not morose. "Plessi's gone," she said, echoing my words, which now had new meaning.

I handed her the newspaper, and she asked me to wait while she read it. She said that Plessi had not known how to swim. "Il ne savait pas nager." She said that not long after he'd arrived in St-Tropez, she'd taken him to the private pool at Hôtel Byblos, where she had a membership. They'd stopped for lunch at La Fégate on rue de la Renaissance, where they'd consumed a litre of wine, and then had downed several drinks at the bar of the Byblos. It was, said Yvette, as though Plessi had been trying to work up his courage. She was surprised, she said, to see him emerge from the men's showers in his rented boxer trunks, bearing all the soap and shampoo he could carry. In the shallow end, he'd lathered himself, splashing and cavorting, until the flabbergasted pool attendant, who was not a lifeguard but a dispenser of towels and plastic bathing caps, had rushed over and yelled at him, telling him he was breaking the law and contaminating the entire pool. He'd have to get out immediately, or else security guards would be summoned and he'd suffer legal consequences. Plessi had willingly complied, saying it didn't matter to him, as he couldn't swim anyway. Unfortunately, as a result of this fiasco, Yvette's membership had been revoked.

She would have kept the newspaper, but I said I wanted it as a souvenir. Reluctantly, she gave it back. She asked if Plessi's apartment at Filles du Soleil had been rented, and I said I didn't know. Would I walk there with her and find out?

117

I said I'd be glad to, but why was she interested? Just to see it, she said. To pay her respects, as she would at a shrine. Perhaps leave a memento, a wreath or something, for old time's sake. If a new tenant had already moved in, she wouldn't bother. But just in case.

It felt strange, walking up quai Suffren with her, past le Relais des Coches, Café des Arts, and Le Gorille. From a flower basket on a table at La Marine, she plucked two roses, a red one and a white one, and placed them in her handbag. Marius, Baptiste and Antoine watched us go by, dangled their hands in that sarcastic, limp-wristed French gesture that pretends to indicate shock. "Monsieur et dame," they called out, "où allez-vous à si grande vitesse?" Where are you going in such a hurry?

The door of Plessi's apartment was locked, so we went and asked Monsieur Nemours for the key. He obviously knew Yvette, was surprised to see her there. At first he said no, we couldn't have the key. A prospective tenant was coming in an hour. Besides, he had no intention of allowing Yvette or anyone else to turn Filles du Soleil into a brothel. To which Yvette reacted angrily, saying this wasn't why she'd come, that Monsieur Nemours had tasted enough of her crêpes to know it was not her style. Nor was I a client of hers. Never had been. Not once. Had I been, we would have gone to my room, not Plessi's. No, she'd come to pay her respects to a dead person, nothing more. Was Monsieur Nemours too crass to understand that?

So finally he gave us the key.

It was weird, not to say spooky, to enter that sanctum. To see Plessi's desk at the window, where he'd laboured long hours every night. And the three-quarter wooden bed on which he'd slept during the day, with water lilies carved on its headboard. There was no physical trace of him, no clothing in the closet, no sign he'd ever been there, yet I think both Yvette and I felt his presence. On the far wall was a large drawing of a mastodon. Beside it, a mirror, and beside that a framed photograph of Notre Dame de Paris at night, with the lights of Ile St-Louis reflected in the Seine, not far from where Plessi's body had been found.

Yvette opened the shutters, stood looking down at the harbour. Then she sat on the bed, and out of her handbag took the two roses and placed them on the rough grey blanket. Only then did she say life was a bitch and begin to cry very softly. Not like a woman in mourning, but like someone whose favourite uncle has died. I sat down on the bed beside her, put my arm around her shoulder. We sat there, feeling the breeze from the window, listening to harbour sounds, marina sounds. People calling to each other across the water. Children shouting. A church bell. A siren. And then, although I don't know how it happened, we were kissing. Not like lovers, exactly, but not like brother and sister either. Before I knew it, we'd taken off most of our clothes. There, on Plessi's bed, on his rough grey blankets, crushing the two roses, I began to comprehend exactly what he'd meant by Yvette's "exceptional services." No doubt about it, she was extraordinary. The thing that amazed me was how noisy we were, making no effort to be circumspect. It was as though we'd both forgotten why we'd come. This was not how one behaved at a wake, at a memorial. Over the mad squeaking of the bedspring, I thought I heard Yvette sobbing, but when I looked at her face, there were no tears. I could imagine Plessi laughing, clapping his hands. "Finally, mon gars! You lose your inhibition! Is Yvette Chanteloup not something? She give you all you can stand, and then some. Did I tell you the truth?"

I don't know how long we were there, in his room, on his bed. I lost track of time. The breeze on our steaming bodies was mildly refreshing. The wind off the sea had grown damp, but not unpleasant. It had started to rain. I was perfectly content, drained, exhausted, listening to Yvette breathing, thinking she'd have to walk back to the Crêperie without an umbrella. As for me, I'd soon be down at Le Gorille, rain or shine, saying goodbye to Marius, sipping my last rum grog of the winter. After that, with my knapsack beside me in a 2nd class compartment, I'd be on my way to Bourg-en-Bresse, with a change of trains at Grenoble and another at Lyon.

At that exact moment the door of Plessi's room burst open and there stood the concierge, Monsieur Nemours, and an elderly couple I'd never seen before. They said something to Monsieur Nemours in German, I think, or it might have been Dutch. Yvette, lying half on me, had her eyes open, but made no move to get up. "Putain!" Monsieur Nemours shouted at her. "C'est expressément, formellement interdit de faire le sport dans ces lieux. C'est pas un bordel!" Harlot! Sex is expressly forbidden on these premises! It's not a bordello!

I'm not sure what he expected us to do. Stand up naked, all stained and sticky? Say we were sorry. If he hadn't had the prospective tenants with him, it might have been less awkward. As it was, they all stood staring at us, especially the German couple, if that's what they were, their eyes fairly popping out of their heads. Still, they didn't appear overly embarrassed. Finally the old woman smiled, cast her eyes about the two bare rooms, told Monsieur Nemours in curiously accented French that this would suit them perfectly. The apartment was entirely suitable, just what they'd been searching for. These days, first class hotels were ridiculously expensive, especially on the French Riviera. And was it really true, as Monsieur Nemours had claimed in his sales pitch, that Guy de Maupassant, F. Scott Fitzgerald, and Jean-Paul Sartre had all lived here? Not at the same time, obviously, but in this very apartment? Fascinating, if true. Her husband, in blue suit and white shoes, less impressed with literary things, was staring fixedly at Yvette. Couldn't take his eyes off her. Before they departed, his wife stepped into the room and called out, "Vive le sport, les athlètes! Vive les jeux olympiques!" Long live sport, you athletes. Long live the Olympic games!

When they were gone, Yvette and I got dressed, closed the shutters, walked downstairs from Plessi's room holding hands. She was crying again, and my own eyes were moist. I debated telling her that by midnight I'd be in Bourg-en-Bresse, at the Hôtel Terminus, in search of her cousin, Iseult. But I didn't. I said, "Don't cry, Yvette. If Plessi were here, he wouldn't want you to cry." The rain had let up enough for us to walk back to Crêperie Bretonne without getting drenched. I wondered if Yvette would be surprised to discover I'd left without saying goodbye, the way Plessi had done. Or perhaps, intuitively, she knew. "Plessi Toussaint est mort," she said as we kissed goodbye and shook hands, in the French manner. "Vive Plessi!" Plessi Toussaint is dead. Long live Plessi.

By the time I got back to Le Gorille, it was raining again. I sat outside anyway, under an umbrella. I had an hour to kill before train time. My knapsack was already packed. I had nothing left to do. My hands barely trembled. Things looked promising. I ordered a rum grog from Marius, who leered at me, called me Casanova, said he hoped for my sake I'd used protection. I told him Yvette had insisted on it. As had her cousin, Iseult. Caution ran in the family. Then I asked him for pen and paper, so I could write down some thoughts before I forgot them. He said how terrible he felt about Plessi's death, could scarcely believe it. Why was it that the best, most generous people died? He said that not seeing Plessi at his usual table would be tragic. He kept expecting to see him, hoping to see him, yet knew it was impossible. He said St-Tropez would never be the same. He asked me if I'd heard about the accident on the Port-Grimaud highway during the night. I said I hadn't. It seems a car from Ramatuelle had collided with one from St-Martin-du-Var and both drivers were in the St-Tropez hospital. People drove too fast on N98, he said, with all its curves and hills. The driver from St-Martin-du-Var, a man named Bricourt, was the brother of Madame Jean-Goujon, proprietor of the book shop at Filles du Soleil. Indeed, Monsieur Bricourt had been on his way to see her when the accident occurred. Now it was doubtful he'd survive. St-Tropez would be in mourning, because Madame

Jean-Goujon was well liked. Father Le Coz had visited her at home. Her husband, Monsieur Jean-Goujon, was in the shipping business and had arranged for Marius to go aboard a French cruise ship, the *Etoile de Champagne*, sailing from Cherbourg to South America twice a year. He would start off as a dining room waiter and rise perhaps to the position of chief steward, which would be better than serving pastis and profiteroles to faded movie stars who never tipped. Speaking of tips, Plessi Toussaint had given him 100 Euros. Was that not generous? For good service and friendship on so many mornings, and the offer, never accepted, of reasonably priced ganja from Morocco. Why, he wondered, was Plessi Toussaint not an advocate of cannabis? He could well have afforded the asking price. He'd once told Marius that such numbing drugs were the worst thing for a working author because they robbed him of his *acuité*, whatever that meant. Still, Plessi Toussaint was a fine man, a fine writer, a fine tipper. It's too bad he was misunderstood and that such bad things were said about him. Things that could hurt him no longer, because he was dead. Marius said he was glad to be leaving St-Tropez and going aboard a ship. I pointed at his wedding ring and asked him what his wife thought about it. He said she'd never know because he wouldn't tell her. The last time he'd visited her in Grenoble, she was living with another man. She hated St-Tropez, had always hated it. Refused to live there, especially in summer. Why, he wondered, if she'd been dissatisfied, could she not have been like big-hearted Yvette Chanteloup, a girl who loved many men equally, but none to the exclusion of others. A girl whose nature it was to please people, not only with her crêpes (though that was important), but with her other asset, her body. As for Marius, he went where the good jobs were, the high-paying jobs, and now was going aboard the luxurious *Etoile de Champagne*. Perhaps some day, if I ever took a voyage from Cherbourg to South America, we would meet again.

As he left to go and serve other tables, sail-boats were heading out to sea. Gulls clamoured. Beyond the lighthouse, the Greek cruise ship *Olympia* had anchored and the first tourists of the season were eager to storm the beaches.

"Plessi Toussaint is dead," I wrote. "Long live Plessi."

Yvette had said it perfectly.

❂

Henri Barrage

The Olympia

Quebec, Canada
2003